COMANCHE, P.I.

COMANCHE, P.I.

Pedro Medina León

Jitney Books

INDEX

La calle es una selva de cemento

Y de fieras salvajes, cómo no

Ya no hay quien salga loco de contento

Donde quiera te espera lo peor

Donde quiera te espera lo peor

In memory of Rafael Laos.

CIUDAD MALDITA

1.

The Romero Detective agency was located on the second floor of an office complex painted in the muted yellows of a *flan* pudding on Flagler Avenue. The stale smell of its carpets barely masked by the misting of a cinnamon-scented Glade air freshener.

"Take a seat." Romero welcomed Comanche, sitting at his desk, dressed in sporty velour behind the rising steam of a fresh *café con leche*.

"It's inconsiderate of you to wake me at 7:30 on a Sunday morning."

"You stink of alcohol, Comanche."

"That's not your problem, it's the weekend," said

Comanche through cottonmouth, glassy eyes and a forehead pockmarked with beads of sweat.

Before heading to the agency, under the warm stream of water in his shower as the foam of his mentholated shampoo slithered down his back and chest, Comanche tried to take inventory of his previous night at the Aruba. Only a few, disjointed images surfaced: low necklines, nearly empty glasses with cigarette butts floating in them, Heineken bottles, trips to the bathroom with his little platinum package containing that white powder that made his heart race and filled him with bravado. At the end—that much was clear—the last round was on the house, courtesy of his friend, the bartender, Tony el Vasco, who squared the register and balanced the accounts behind closed doors, Hector Lavoe songs playing in the background.

Officer Pérez from Miami Beach PD, Romero's old colleague, had called to ask for his services. He did it every time they needed meticulous work or to conceal something from making the news. This time it was a little bit of both: they found a body, Gregorio Lizárraga, 38, on the Venetian Causeway sometime that morning. It occurred in a rich area; it would be better for the MBPD if the crime didn't attract attention. No gunshot or stab wounds, a fracture at the base of his cranium, but with numerous struggle marks around his neck and along his arms. No wallet, ID or cell phone, just a backpack with a notebook in which the outline for a story was written, character descriptions and sketches for scenes. On the first page, his name. After a quick inquiry, they'd found he worked at La Chismosa, a Taqueria on Washington Avenue.

In an exclusive neighborhood like the Venetian, an explanation had to be given to nosy neighbors who enjoyed the relative privacy of their barrier island community between Downtown Miami and Miami Beach. It had been a couple, out for an early walk, who alerted the police at five in the morning. Romero placed printouts of Lizárraga's photos across his desk that he'd received from Officer Pérez via email. He had already booked the little motel on Alton Road that Comanche liked; it was best for him to arrive in Miami Beach that same afternoon and start the case first thing Monday morning. Here he had three hundred-dollar bills for his meals. Comanche didn't mind the idea of getting lost among the palm trees, the turquoise sea, and the beach tourists, and he complied without complaining.

"Give me a call at the end of every day."

"That's it?"

"Yeah, why?"

"The info on Lizárraga is not enough to go on. Where did he live?"

"Negative Comanche, we don't have an address."

"Find it."

"Not today, I'll square that with Pérez."

"Any prints?"

"You'll have to wait a couple of days on that and any DNA."

"So, all we got is that Gregorio Lizárraga hit the pavement and died from a blow to the occipital lobe as a result of a struggle."

"Affirmative."

2.

After starting his day off in the muted yellows of Romero's *flan* pudding office, Comanche crossed over on the Macarthur Causeway with its uninterrupted views of Fisher Island and docked transatlantic cruise ships filling up with passengers dreaming of Caribbean paradises. Entering Miami Beach, he stopped at a red light on Alton Road next to a convertible Mini Cooper filled with attractive twentysomethings, their faces covered with Gucci and Dior shades. It was like transitioning from Hell to Heaven.

The clerk at the El Bikini motel was playing Candy Crush on his iPhone when Comanche appeared at the desk behind his Ray Bans and holding a small bag.

"Yoooo, maaaaan!" he said, not surprised.

"What's up, Skinny?" replied Comanche.

"Good, good. Haven't seen you in a while."

"About five months, maybe less. Maybe not that many."

Skinny removed a keyring from a small wooden plank that hung on the wall behind him next to a windowsill that had a pair of impromptu vases made from Sprite bottles. He had the same room available as always, at the end of the hallway, second door on the right, smoking allowed and with an espresso maker and hot plate inside. It had been vacant when Romero called that morning and Skinny'd gotten La Cara de Trapo to clean it.

Comanche set his bag on the bed and before heading out to get a bottle of Bacardí and a tin of Bustelo coffee, he lit a Marlboro and sat on the toilet to check his messages. Both were from Romero: Pérez would come by El Bikini later and drop off some photos of Lizárraga and copies of what was written in his notebooks. The second message said he'd forgotten to mention in his previous text that the forensic results would be ready the next day. He replied, once again asking for Lizárraga's address, and Romero fired back to check his messages. He already had it.

3.

Comanche had a cup of Bustelo and a cigarette for breakfast before he headed out to Gregorio Lizárraga's home, an efficiency on 9th Street and Meridian Avenue, a modest spot he was able to enter after jiggling the lock. It was small, small for an efficiency even, with a tiny bath, a little hot stove in the corner, bed, and in front of the bed, a small table stacked with books, notebooks, scribblings, and on the wall, next to the table, a corkboard covered in tacked papers.

Comanche took some down, they were numbered. On these, like the notebook they'd found him, was the flow of a story beginning to take shape and some character descriptions. One of these, unlike the others, had numbers and a tally of monthly bills: rent, cellphone, Publix, electric, and at the end, marked with a bold "X," it said 'owed = $800.' Then he checked what little there was to check under the bed and all he came up with was a small mound of socks, underwear, t-shirts and pants. It wouldn't be worth his time to spend another minute there.

4.

He'd eaten at La Chismosa on Washington before and since his breakfast had been sparse, a coffee and a smoke, he ordered the *al pastor* tacos while he waited out the ten minutes the manager had asked for before meeting with him.

"Any sauce or pico de gallo?" asked the man at the counter.

"Tomatillo."

"Wanna make it a combo?"

"What comes with it?"

"Chips and a soda."

"Ok."

Comanche sat at a table next to the big window looking out on Washington. Outside, the bustling parade of enhanced, king sized asses and convertibles banging out hip hop tracks had not begun. If anything, Miami Beach looked more like the pleasant, sleepy seaside community that had once been dubbed "God's Waiting Room" with its soft red sidewalks and palm trees slowly swaying in the breeze.

"Sorry about that, Inspector," said the manager, drying his hands on his apron. "Cabalito, at your service."

"Nice to meet you," said Comanche through a mouthful of tortilla chips drenched in tomatillo sauce. "Have a seat."

It had been a string of crazy days; his cashier had quit unexpectedly and the guy he had at the register as a replacement had no idea what he was doing. He'd just fucked a delivery order for huevos rancheros and Cabalito had to go into the kitchen to sort the mess out, hence the ten-minute wait. "Fucking ingrates the lot of them, they're all the same in this shithole town," said Cabalito. "They leave you high and dry for 25 cents more, it's not the first time this happened."

Comanche slid Lizárraga's photo across the table.

"That the cashier who didn't come back?"

"That's the son of a bitch."

"He's dead."

Not the words Cabalito expected as he raised his hands to his face and covered his eyes. He couldn't believe it. Comanche explained that was the reason why he was there. Lizárraga had been found on the Venetian Causeway Sunday morning and he needed Cabalito to tell him everything and anything about him. Down to the smallest detail.

"Can we go outside for a smoke?" asked Cabalito. "My stomach's upset."

The last time he had seen Lizárraga alive had been at the La Chismosa around seven p.m. on Saturday after he finished his shift. Cabalito couldn't think of where he'd go after, but he normally went back to his efficiency to write. All Lizárraga dreamt of was to become a writer and had been working on a novel. Even if he did stop at the Al Capone bar from time to time for a beer or two, he always went straight home to write. At least that's what he said at the taco stand. That past week though, some bullshit had come up between him and a coworker.

"When during the week?" interrupted Comanche. "Exactly when?"

"Uh, lemme see," stammered Cabalito.

At the taco stand worked a young, attractive Argentine named Karina who was well-liked by everyone since she was the only woman on the crew. Everyone showed her respect and she reciprocated, but Cabalito had noticed that there was something between her and Lizárraga. Karina was an avid reader and would frequently ask Lizárraga for recommendations or what he thought about this author or another; they'd take their breaks together and sit in the alley smoking and talking about books.

"Where is she now?"

"I'm getting to that," said Cabalito as he flicked his Lucky Strike ash away.

Friday, around Karina and Lizárraga's end of shift, Karina's boyfriend had turned up at the taco stand asking for Lizárraga who was at the time taking out the trash back in the alley. When he came back in, he went to the boyfriend and asked, servilely, how he could be of help. The response he got was a shove and a threat: "Stay away from my girl, you son of a bitch, or I'll kill you." Karina had been in the back office, clocking out, and had not heard the loud exchange out front, but exited as Lizárraga stood his own and demanded to know who the fuck did that piece of shit think he was to threaten him like that. Between Cabalito and Karina they calmed the two down and everyone left their separate ways. A couple of hours later, Cabalito got a message from Karina saying she was sorry about the scene, and she asked if she could get the week off. The scuffle left her feeling triggered and she would need some time to square away her affairs so it wouldn't happen again. When Lizárraga failed to show up at La Chismosa, Cabalito called Karina since he was short-staffed. He called her a handful of times with no answer, the calls went straight to voicemail.

"You got an address for her?"

"No, man. We don't ask for addresses or papers here of the employees, you know how it is with *la migra*."

"Boyfriend's name?"

"Runcho. El Runcho, that's what he goes by."

"That a first or last name?"

"I think his name is Juan, I think but I'm not sure. Runcho is the last name."

"I'll need an address and the name, how are we going to get that?"

"Look, I dunno but generally, everyone here lives kinda nearby. Most ride bike."

"Nah, I can't do anything with that, and you can see why it's very important for me to talk with her after what you've described."

"I'll think about how I can help," Cabalito said. "Wait for my call, you can count on that."

"And another thing."

"What?"

"Do you know if Lizárraga maybe had some money issues?" asked Comanche, the list of utilities and debt fresh on his mind.

"No, not that I know of, but I can't think he would've told me something like that."

"Thanks."

Comanche walked towards the corner, making sure Cabalito stayed behind and was out of his line of sight. He sat at a bus stop, next to a homeless man. The sidewalk was flecked with dry vomit. He called Romero back after seeing a text message asking him to do so.

"Romero."

"Alcohol and weed in the blood, according to the forensics report Officer Pérez just sent."

"Good."

"Turn anything up on your end, Comanche?"

"Not yet, but I'm following a lead."

5.

El Ilusiones was like a second home for Comanche: behind its counter, Consorte prepared peppery fried eggs and Cuban toasts that bled copious amounts of butter when pressed. He always had Héctor Lavoe blasting from the speakers and thanks to his comings and goings in Miami Beach's underworld, was Comanche's trusted informant. But if there was one thing inside El Ilusiones that made him feel even more comfortable than anywhere else, was its pool table. He could spend hours there, sucking down Marlboro after Marlboro, striking the cue ball, delighting in the way it crashed into the colored ones atop the wasted felt marked by years of careless smokers.

"Let's see if you can put some real music on," said Comanche as he slid atop one of the stools at the counter.

From the grease covered speakers on the corners a voice sang: *¿Qué es lo que hace un taxista seduciendo a la vida? ¿Qué es lo que hace un taxista construyendo una herida?*

"Fuck! My brotha!" said Consorte as he put aside the two glasses he had just dried with his towel. "Let me touch you and see if you're real, you've been lost my man!"

"Cut it out bro, that's a bit much."

"Been a couple months, my brotha, at least four or five. Other day Chamizo was here, and we were talking about you and your ingratitude."

"Hey, I haven't had any business on this side of the water."

"Anyways… fried eggs with pepper?"

"No thanks, just ate at La Chismosa," said Comanche as he took out an envelope with Lizárraga's photos.

"Who's that? The 'Dead of the Day?'"

Gregorio Lizárraga. Argentine national. Cashier at La

Chismosa. Lived in an efficiency on 9th Street and Meridian. Writer, or at least intended to be one. Body found on the Venetian Sunday morning, no gunshot or stab wounds. Died from cranial trauma. Possibly from impacting the pavement. Alcohol and weed in him. At first glance it looked like a robbery since his wallet wasn't found, but he'd have to dive deeper into it since Officer Pérez and Romero asked. That's why Comanche would need Consorte's help.

Consorte couldn't think of anyone who'd know anything, but he'd make some calls. Surely, he'd find something. The crew from a local rag, *Revólver*, were regulars for breakfast at El Ilusiones, if Lizárraga was a writer, there was a chance they'd cross paths in the Beach's literary scene.

"Yeah, that could work. I have fuck all to go with."

Diners walked in and Consorte excused himself. Comanche lit a cigarette as he walked over to the pool table, sucking in the smoke gently as he arranged the balls in the triangle, Lavoe's *"Periódico de ayer"* on the speakers. He broke, sinking the red ball in the left corner pocket. Now he put his aim on yellow, sinking it in the same hole. Later he got Cabalito's call, the manager had turned something up. He walked out of El Ilusiones with a wink toward Consorte, letting him know he'd see him real soon.

One of the girls who worked at the restaurant next to La Chismosa sometimes walked home with Karina since they lived on the same block of small apartments and efficiencies in front of Flamingo Park. They'd be easy to find, their obnoxious pink exteriors standing out among the softer pastels of the neighborhood. Cabalito had written the address on a napkin telling him he'd been having a hard time since hearing the news. "He was a good kid, responsible, never complained about working extra hours, whatever time he was needed." He wanted Comanche to keep him informed, adding "El Runcho is Juan, Juan Runcho."

6.

Comanche knocked on Karina's door a couple of times and no one answered but noticing a slight movement in the curtains, he insisted, raising his license to the window.

"I need to speak with Karina, now, before things get… complicated."

The lock turned, opening on a tired looking blonde, her hair tied halfway back, barefoot, wearing t-shirt and Adidas sweatpants.

"Can I help you?"

"Are you Karina?"

"Yes."

"Can I come in?"

"What's this about?"

"This," said Comanche as he showed her the photo of Lizárraga sprawled on the Venetian, his open eyes gazing into the heavens. "Mr. Gregorio Lizárraga is dead."

The room was warm and smelled like it had been batted down and shut for days, no trace of fresh air or light in the scent. Plates with dried rice were stacked in the sink and an empty coffee mug on the nightstand. The bed sheets were tussled, the pillows dented, books littered the floor all around the bed and there was a small table with a pair of red chairs.

"Sit, if you'd like," she said, wiping the quiet tears that began to stream down her face.

Comanche nodded in acceptance, taking off his aviators and hanging them on his shirt collar.

"What happened? When did this happen? she asked, amid sobs.

"Saturday night," Comanche said. "Between Saturday night and Sunday morning." He informed her that he'd been to La Chismosa and spoken to Cabalito who told him she was friends with Lizárraga and that there had been a problem with her boyfriend Runcho. He wanted her to tell him everything, everything she could about Lizárraga.

El Runcho was a jealous asshole, there wasn't a single thing he hadn't caused her problems with, and they'd been together for a year, living there. He'd moved in after a couple of months of dating. They had met at Flamingo Park; she'd lay on a blanket reading after work, and he'd be playing tennis with his friends. When he moved in, he'd just lost his job at a Brazilian cafeteria that had closed. Then, she confessed out of the desperation of being over the loser, that he'd leave early every day to play tennis and waste the day away at the park. Not looking for work, eating out all the time, going to Heat games, buying new Nikes on Lincoln Road, the newest Play Station. Turns out the tennis thing was a lie, he and his buddies sold coke at the park and had been doing so for a long time. He had never worked in a

Brazilian cafeteria; his clients texted him when they pulled up to the park and he or one of his buddies would walk up to the car and make the sale in the blink of an eye.

"Wait, wait a minute," Comanche interrupted. "As far as I know, El Runcho is your boyfriend, why are you telling me this?"

"No, see? Look," Karina said as she raised her t-shirt, showing him her belly and back. "Look how the asshole left me, it's not the first time."

El Runcho had whipped her, the red welts across her flesh speaking to the savagery of his attack.

"When did he do that?"

"Last Saturday night."

"Same day Lizárraga was killed," Comanche said, asking Karina for a glass of water.

"That's it."

"At what time did he do that? Could he have beat you then gone out looking for Lizárraga?"

"I don't know the time, exactly, but I think it was around midnight. I don't know if he went out looking for Lizárraga, I took a Rivotril and went to sleep. All I know for sure is that he was in bed, next to me, the following morning."

"Where is he now?"

"He went out Sunday morning and hasn't been back. Said he needed to clear his mind and that if I went back to La Chismosa, there'd be consequences."

"You know where he might be?" asked Comanche, taking a long swallow that drained the glass. He pulled out his packet of smokes, asking if he could light up. Karina said yes and walked over to get the empty mug from the nightstand, placing it between the two of them on the table.

"No clue, I haven't seen him by the tennis courts, him or his friends."

"What are their names? His friends, you know where I can find them?"

"I've never even spoken to any of them. All I know is that

one is Argentinian, they call him Fiorito, and the other they call Da Vinci. But nothing else. When I met Runcho, he'd be the only one who'd come to me, and he never bothered to introduce them to me."

"I'll assume Da Vinci is Italian?"

"No, he uses a *vincha*, a headband, part of the tennis outfit look."

"Gregorio Lizárraga, tell me about him," said Comanche pulling on his cigarette before exhaling a silky plume of smoke. "I'm listening."

They had met at La Chismosa, working the same morning shift. The taco stand got busy for lunch but since they served breakfast, they opened early. Breakfast service was slow, but Cabalito was convinced his huevos rancheros were a hit, so there they were to take orders. They had hit it off immediately. She was from Mar del Plata, and he was from Buenos Aires, and they both loved Argentine authors. They both loved reading. And he wrote, a crazy dreamer who thought he'd become an author in Miami – not Madrid, Mexico City, or even his beloved Buenos Aires – but Miami, the most anti-literate city on the planet. He would tell her about the novel he was working on, *Ciudad Maldita*, giving her bits of it to read. They'd spend hours talking about *Ciudad Maldita* and other books. Downtime at La Chismosa was never enough so they'd take their breaks together or go outside to the alleyway for a quick hit of a joint.

"Karina," Comanche interrupted, "Aside from Runcho being violent, did he have real reasons to be jealous of Lizárraga?"

She turned her face, blushing. The last time she'd been at Lizárraga's efficiency, she'd forgotten her jean jacket, a Gap jacket, and her hairband. She'd left that on the sink, when she cleaned up and put on her panties and bra. She was scared that they'd make a connection with Lizárraga, now that they were investigating.

"I visited his place," said Comanche, smoking. "I did not see these items."

"They are in the closet, in a Publix bag," said Karina. "Or so he said."

Comanche understood and told her he'd remove the jacket and hairband, but she'd have to leave the efficiency before El Runcho returned. She said she had nowhere to go. He said he'd ask the cops to keep watch and gave her his number, that he'd be a phone call away, 24 hours a day. To call him for anything, no matter how insignificant it seemed, he'd be over immediately.

"Man, I'm all fucked up over this, it's just hitting me."

"I'm sorry. You know how Lizárraga was doing financially?"

"No, no clue. He figured out his month to month like anyone, I guess. Why?"

Comanche chose not to mention the list he'd taken from the corkboard, understanding that the guy had a debt, saying it was 'procedure' and wanted to rule out that the victim had financial problems as it was one of the main reasons people got killed.

"No, the truth is, like I said, he never talked or complained about that."

"You got a photo of Runcho?"

She showed him a photo of the couple on her cellphone, no doubt from better times, at a bar on Española Way, toasting with mojitos.

"Another thing."

"Yes?"

"Did Lizárraga have any family over here?"

Not that she knew of. He was divorced, his marriage ending in Argentina due to the long distance and for some other issue that according to Lizárraga, was some kind of shame he never spoke of.

Comanche walked around Flamingo Park, Runcho's photo fresh on his mind, but he was nowhere to be seen, or Fiorito or Da Vinci. Maybe he'd done enough for the day he thought, he still had to pass by Lizárraga's efficiency to grab Karina's things. He'd then get himself a two-liter of Coca-Cola, make himself some Fiestas in the quiet of El Bikini.

"Go ahead, Comanche," answered Romero.

"You got anything on the prints and DNA?"

"Nothing yet, what about on your end?"

"Write this down: Juan Runcho."

It was of utmost importance that Pérez ran that name. The day before Lizárraga's death, Runcho had threatened him, and he vanished Sunday. Comanche had just interviewed his girlfriend and found out that he was violent, beat her, and made a living on the Beach with his pals dealing coke out of Flamingo Park.

"What a gem," said Romero.

"What would be ideal," Comanche said, "would be for Pérez and his men to run a search on him too."

If Miami Beach PD had anyone available, they'd do it, but the department was short-staffed and wouldn't prioritize a minor case like this. All the major crime that entered

Miami, did so through Miami Beach: mountains of coke, human trafficking, prostitution. In short, all resources went to combating that.

Comanche walked the few blocks over to Lizárraga's place. As he finished jiggling the lock, he was struck with something upside his head and buckled over, dropping down in such a way that he couldn't see who had hit him as they ran out into the darkness of Meridian Avenue. It took him a minute to get his footing back, raising his hand slowly to feel a growing bump that radiated pain as he barely grazed it with his fingertips. He finished getting up as best he could and started towards Karina's apartment. She was surprised to see him back so quickly. He told her what had just happened, afraid that Runcho had been the one to beat him.

"You want ice?" she asked as she returned to her stove where she was cooking spaghetti in tomato sauce.

"Yeah, if it's not too much trouble," Comanche said.

"Did you retrieve the bag?" said Karina. "With my clothes?"

"Negative."

"Shit."

"Relax. You have nothing to fear."

"So, says you."

Comanche noted that the food smelled good. "You cook that gravy from scratch?"

"Nah, it's Ragu, from a jar, all I did was add a little oregano and pepper."

"Throw a little sugar and laurel in there."

"Oh, you cook too?"

"When I can." At the hostel where Comanche lived in Little Havana, he had a small kitchen next to his bathroom even though he usually took all his meals at the counter at La Carreta, which doubled as his office, in a way. There he figured out his cases while enjoying the endless ebb-and-flow of waiters and waitresses, their trays stacked with plates, glasses, coming in-and-out of the kitchen. On Saturdays, before his routine bar hops that always ended shipwrecked and comatose at the Aruba, he'd be in that little kitchen, cooking up a steak with thick rings of onions and tomatoes in low heat, or some pork chops. Sometimes some pasta.

Karina turned her stove off, covered the pot, and wrapped some ice cubes in a small rag. Comanche checked his phone as the cold penetrated his skin, blasting his brain. He had a message from Consorte: meet me tomorrow, early, at El Ilusiones.

He'd found something interesting.

7.

How many hours had he slept? Nine, ten? Unusual for him. He had trouble stringing four hours of sleep in a row, but that hit took a lot out of him. Karina had been kind enough to ice him down which made the pain tolerable and reduced the swelling. She served him a plate of pasta too so he wouldn't return to El Bikini with an empty stomach. Comanche turned on the coffeemaker, and as the aroma of Bustelo began to fill the room, he got under a hot shower and lathered up with Head and Shoulders, the foam running down his body, down to his balls. It relaxed him to massage himself like that, certainly longer than needed, but it had become a routine. He got to El Ilusiones at 10 a.m., sat at the bar and asked Consorte to fry up some eggs, extra pepper, Cuban toast, and a black coffee – his second that day.

"Bro, in about half an hour, one of the *Revólver* guys will be here. He was with Lizárraga Saturday night."

"Before you go on," interrupted Comanche, "I'm going to need to borrow the piece, same as before."

"I have it here, what happened?"

"Got dropped last night," Comanche said, touching the back of his head. "Fuck if I get dropped again, gotta strap, just in case."

"Sure, gimmie a sec."

"Alright, go on."

There wasn't much more, only that he'd gotten in touch with Wild Cat, one of the magazine's editors who'd been with Lizárraga at the Al Capone bar last Saturday night. Maybe he'd have something. Consorte hadn't told him anything other than to come by El Ilusiones to have a coffee with a friend of his who needed a favor.

"Let me get a glass of water."

"Look, there he is," pointing with his chin towards the door.

Wild Cat was an unkempt fellow, uncombed hair, baggy jeans, white t-shirt, Adidas Samba sneakers. Consorte served him a coffee and Cuban toast and introduced him to Comanche, leaving the two alone at a table to talk.

"Let me know if you need me or want anything else."

"Nice to meet you," said Wild Cat, crossing his right leg over his left. "What's good?"

Comanche showed him his PI license and Lizárraga's photo and Wild Cat stared back with a blank expression. "He's dead," Comanche said, and without skipping a beat so Wild Cat wouldn't have time to process, "They killed him Saturday, between Saturday night and Sunday morning to be more exact."

"What the fuck?" exclaimed Wild Cat, his eyes widening. "What's wrong with you, man? The fuck are you telling me?"

Exactly what he had just heard, Comanche told him, immediately asking Wild Cat for all the details about Saturday night and that he knew they'd been together. And he wanted Wild Cat to tell him everything he knew about Lizárraga. Wild Cat couldn't believe it, simply couldn't. He knew little about his personal life, he knew – without much detail – that the divorce had hit him hard, that he was a fellow man of letters and good company, had finished writing his novel, *Ciudad Maldita*, and *Revólver* wanted to publish it through its editorial wing. That's why they had met, the *Revólver* crew hosted a night at the Al Capone bar, "Litertura Callejera" a sort of open mic, magazine and book sale that featured a local rock band bookending the evening. That night it had been La chica más pop de South Beach, their singer was in demand in the city's underground venues and had been gaining notoriety as South Beach's hottest pop chick.

"What did you two talk about, every detail of it?"

"Not much, really. I told him we wanted to publish *Ciudad Maldita*."

"When you say 'we,' who do you mean?" said Comanche, pulling out a cigarette and lighting it, leaving the pack of Marlboros on the table in case Wild Cat wanted one, but with a wave and look of disgust he let Comanche know he hated cigarettes.

Consorte came up to them, excusing himself for the interruption, with a pair of ice-cold Coca-Colas – in glass bottles, Comanche's favorite.

"I mean Lasticön and Ginonzski."

"Right, and who are they?"

"The rest of *Revólver*."

"They talk with him too?"

"No, just me."

"What time did Lizárraga get to the bar?"

"Around 8, that's when 'Litertura Callejera' starts."

"When did he leave?"

"Can't tell for sure. Pistolas Rosadas finished their set at 10, that's when I talked with him about his book, but I don't remember talking with him again after that."

"Lizárraga, was he alone or what?"

"He was with Luigi Lechuga when we talked."

"Who's this Luigi Lechuga?"

"Local guy, part of the scene, never misses an event. Good reader too."

"Can you find him?"

"I guess, I got his number," showing Comanche his phone. "You want it?"

"You call him. Call him now and tell him to come over."

"Uhm, yeah but I've only called him like once or twice before, he's gonna be surprised that I'm calling, to say the least."

"No matter, tell him it's about books."

Wild Cat placed his phone on the table, clicked on speaker, and hit Luigi's number. Lechuga picked up on the second ring.

"Hey man, it's me, Wild Cat."

"Yo, what's up?"

"Yeah bro, can you come by El Ilusiones for a bit?"

"Why's that? What for?"

Comanche gave him a look that said, 'don't fuck this up' and 'be careful' all at once.

"We're thinking about creating a new section in the magazine and we think it'd be right up your alley."

"Oh cool, sure, gimmie a couple of minutes, I'm nearby."

8.

Luigi Lechuga was slim, round-cheeked, puffy even, his hair a curly mop the unsettling shiny color of cockroaches. He wore a Darth Vader print t-shirt, black jeans, and red Converse canvas sneakers. He stank of weed and his left eye was swollen purple. He'd been punched recently. Lechuga put a hand on Wild Cat's back. He was all ears, almost comical the way they stuck out from that mop. Comanche didn't wait for pleasantries, showed him his license and asked him to sit down, telling Wild Cat to stick around and wait at the bar.

"What's this about," asked Lechuga, taken aback. "This some kind of joke, a prank, what's up man?"

"Sit," repeated Comanche as Lechuga remained standing.

He put Lizárraga's photos that he'd kept in his shirt pocket on top of the table. "You know him?"

"Yeah, I know him. Of course, but who are you man?"

"He's dead. Did you know?"

Lechuga laughed. How could he know, he'd just been with him a couple of days ago.

"So, you've spoken with him since?"

Lechuga hesitated, visibly taking inventory of his recent past, finally saying no, that he had not.

"Well, Gregorio Lizárraga is dead. He was killed sometime between Saturday night and Sunday morning, on the Venetian Causeway." Comanche lit up a cigarette and offered one to Lechuga, who mumbled an excuse that he only smoked when he drank but this had gotten him nervous as he reached for the pack of Marlboros in Comanche's outstretched hand.

Like Wild Cat had said, Lechuga and Lizárraga had been together at the Al Capone Saturday night, adding that they'd left together for another drink at Joe's at the Venetian. They had been there before since Luigi worked the midnight shift in the kitchen there. They left Capone's around 10:30, lighting up a joint Lizárraga had on him as he excitedly discussed his book and *Revólver's* interest in publishing it. They sat at the bar in Joe's close to 11, each one ordering a Heineken that they promptly drowned in a pair of gulps and said their goodbyes since Lechuga was about to start his shift. If Lizárraga stuck around after, he wouldn't know since the kitchen was closed off from the main area, but it certainly was a possibility.

"How often did you two go to Joe's together?"

They didn't really go together, apparently Lizárraga liked the bar and went once or twice a week, and Lechuga, on his breaks, would join him for a joint in the alley to ease the night.

"So Lizárraga was known to the bar staff."

"Yeah, for sure."

"You know if he ever had any trouble with anyone there?"

"No, not that I know of."

Comanche's running theory, at the moment, pieced from

these conversations, was that Lizárraga was killed by someone he met at Joe's. His body had been found nearby and the neighborhood was not known for random robberies. In fact, one look at him and anyone could see that he wouldn't have been the target of a robbery, his white t-shirt, jeans and Skechers were of no value.

"Until what time do you work at Joe's?"

"Eleven to 3 a.m., part-time, four hours a night."

"By the time you finish your shift and actually leave the bar, that take a long time?"

"No, not usually. I clock out, take my apron off, hang it, say goodbye… I'd say around ten minutes, max."

"That's around the time he was killed. Did you see him leave?"

"No."

"Didn't see anything strange?"

"No."

"Look at me in my eyes when I speak."

"Sorry."

"You didn't see anyone roaming around when you left?"

"No."

"What did you do after you left?"

"I dunno, go home. I walked home."

"You don't know what you did two nights ago at 3 a.m.?"

"I told you. I walked home."

"How long did that take?"

"Fifteen, 20 minutes, I dunno."

"You don't know shit."

"I don't keep time when I walk."

"You didn't see anyone walking around the Causeway when you left?"

"No, there was no one, I told you, you just asked me the same thing. It's really quiet around there at that time."

"What happened to your eye?"

"I got into a fight."

"With Lizárraga?"

"What's your fucking problem with me man? I'd never get into a fight with him. We were good friends."

"Lizárraga dies from a blow to the head, same time you leave work," Comanche said before gulping down the last of his Coke, settling the glass bottle on the table before letting out a loud belch. "And here you are, with a black eye, bit of a coincidence, don't you think?"

"I don't know, I dunno… shit," Lechuga said, getting red, a thick vein throbbing in his neck.

"You hit him first or did he attack you?"

Lechuga got up, annoyed by the question. He'd had enough of Comanche.

"Did you kill Gregorio Lizárraga sometime between Saturday night and Sunday morning?" continued Comanche.

"You're accusing me? What's your fucking problem?"

"Lower your tone, you little shit," said Comanche with his gaze firmly fixed on Lechuga. "Look at my fucking eyes when I speak, second time I have to tell you."

"Who do you think you are to accuse me of this? I won't stand for this shit," Lechuga said, now fixing his eyes, defiantly, on Comanche.

"You can go," Comanche said, turning towards Wild Cat. "You too. Keep your phones handy and don't leave the Beach, good chance I'll need you both again."

Consorte handed him an Airwalk shoebox, it's where he kept the Glock wrapped in old newspapers. Comanche thanked him, told him he'd have it back in a few days. "Get me black coffee, to the brim, that fucking idiot Lechuga pissed me off. I gotta calm down." The box had some old issues of *Revólver* in it and Consorte told him to look up Wild Cat's articles on Miami's history and pop culture. Maybe there was something in there that could help him.

"Maybe, okay, but I'll be back for them," he said. He'd have to keep investigating after leaving El Ilusiones and it would be hard to do with a shoebox and old magazines under his arm.

"Sure, you're right. I'll hold them but don't forget to come back."

"Count on it, alright bro, I'm out," said Comanche, draining his mug and dabbing his lips with a paper napkin.

Comanche called Romero to find out about the DNA results and if any prints had been lifted. Romero told him they should have them by the afternoon and that he had info on El Runcho from Officer Pérez. Juan Runcho had a rap sheet: marijuana possession, one sexual harassment complaint, and another for domestic violence, and in all these cases he'd been released on bond without any real consequences. No surprise there. However, what was surprising was that they had found his prints in Lizárraga's efficiency, as well as Karina's and Comanche's, but the most recent ones were Comanche's and Runcho's, which confirmed, at least to him, that Runcho had been the one to drop him and tied him directly to Lizárraga's murder. Suspect number one. Before he could ask Romero why they'd gotten the results from the apartment first, and not the body, Romero clarified that this was a simple procedure and that the other information required a forensics report and therefore, more bureaucracy. Pérez had put the arrest order on Runcho – high priority since Runcho dealt coke out of the tennis courts at Flamingo Park and that was an investigation the department had been conducting for a few months at that point. Connecting Runcho to it had been a big break.

"So that was the son of a bitch who got the drop on me, I knew it. Hope they grab him soon and give me five minutes alone with him so I can return the gift in kind."

"How's the investigation going? With Runcho alone on the suspect list this gives us more time to focus on our end."

"You got a paper and pen handy? Write this name down."

"Go ahead."

"Luigi Lechuga."

"What's Lechuga's real name?"

"That's his first and last, far as I know."

"Oh, okay, okay… and why're we after him?"

Comanche had just interrogated him, in a way, and he didn't like the way Lechuga reacted. Agitated, doubtful, he kept looking at the floor or around the room and he had a black eye that could've happened during a fight with Gregorio Lizárraga. He'd also been one of the last known people to see Lizárraga alive, they'd been together at the bar where Lechuga worked, they drank beer together. Lechuga left to clock in for his shift and Lizárraga stayed behind at the bar, drinking some more. According to Lechuga, Lizárraga was a regular at the bar, so he'd have to go by the bar later, see if he could reconstruct Lizárraga's last minutes, since he had apparently walked out alive before being murdered, literally, around the corner. Lechuga's story didn't sit right with Comanche: he'd left work and walked home, same time as the murder took place, and wasn't it convenient he didn't notice anything out of the ordinary, or even Lizárraga's body on the street. Strange. Very strange, considering the time and that the way to his house would've been on the same sidewalk that Gregorio Lizárraga's body lay. And the black eye.

"What's the name of the bar?"

"Joe's at the Venetian."

"Listen, Comanche, we should reconstruct the scene entirely and find out if Runcho was also there that night."

"Absolutely, now that his prints place him at Lizárraga's, but we gotta get Lechuga on the radar as well."

"Agreed, I'll see if Pérez can get a warrant for the cameras at Joe's."

"Best if that can be done today."

"I'm on it."

9.

Karina was about to get in the shower. She'd been out for a run at the park on South Point. She was sweating still, her tight leggings hugging a round and firm ass Comanche had not seen the previous afternoon. He apologized if it wasn't a good time and that he could come back later, but Karina invited him inside.

"How's your head?"

"Better."

"You want something to drink?"

"Water please," he asked. "When will you be back at La Chismosa?"

Karina didn't want to go back there. She was a trained

bartender and was looking for bartending work. She had enough saved up to last a couple of months, but she'd been talking to a few bars and one of them, the Al Capone, was looking like they'd make her a job offer. She was happy about that because the bar was one of the hottest on the Beach and that meant more tips.

Comanche wanted to talk more about Runcho, that's why he'd come. They sat at the small table, on the red chairs, two glasses of water between them. It looked like she had tidied up the place. El Runcho had that rap sheet, the domestic violence, sexual harassment, the weed charge, and his prints had been found at Lizárraga's place the day Comanche had been knocked down. He wanted Karina to tell him everything she knew about the charges.

"Wait, wait a minute, wait… you're coming into my home to call me a liar?" She was offended.

"No, chill," Comanche said. "I've been in this shit long

enough to know that sometimes, whether they're afraid of the abuser, or the cops, people don't talk."

"No, everything I told you before is true."

The police were out looking for him, his priors, added to the threats he made at La Chismosa and entering the dead man's efficiency fingered him as the primary suspect. And that was without Karina's story of the whipping and his illegal comings and goings at Flamingo Park. Comanche could only speculate, given what little he knew, but Runcho's coke business at the park smelled like a big fish for the police.

"Best you can do is get out of this place," Comanche said, reminding her of his previous advice. "Somewhere safe where that son of a bitch can't find you. I bet he's around, just waiting for us to drop our guard."

"I don't have a lot of options," she said. "My friend Kina has her cousin, who just got here, in her efficiency now. She'd be the only one I could ask for something like that."

"I asked you before, about Lizárraga's finances, remember?"

asked Comanche, taking out the note from Lizárraga's wall from his wallet, showing it to her. "It was because of this."

"Nah man, no clue. He'd been through a divorce," she reminded him. He'd never gone into details but had mentioned some sort of tragedy. She thought maybe there was something there, if anything.

"Hmm. Maybe. Well, best we stay in touch," Comanche said as he got up from the chair. "I left you my number before, right?"

"Yeah, thanks," she said as she walked him to the door. "I'm sorry if I'm acting funny."

"Don't sweat it, you're in a tough spot," he said as he raised a Marlboro to his lips. Then he put on his black Ray Ban aviators.

10.

Comanche had a message from Romero on his phone, Officer Pérez had been by El Bikini and left him an envelope with the warrant for Joe's cameras, so he headed straight for the motel, where Skinny, immersed in the inane pastime of Candy Crush or Minecraft on his iPhone, greeted him at the desk and gave him the envelope. In his room, the remnants of disinfectants and other cleaning products clung hard in the air, a credit to La Cara de Trapo's cleaning prowess. He took the Glock out from his waistband, leaving it on the bed, and walked into the bathroom to sit on the toilet and have a smoke. If there was something that filled him with adrenaline and bit down on him with the strength of addiction, it was investigating.

Once he was involved in one, the blinders came down and his brain blocked everything else. All he could think of was the case and its moving pieces and how they'd help him solve it, but sitting on the toilet put a pause to that whirlwind, and for a moment he wanted to send everything to Hell and lean on the bar at the Aruba, in front of Tony el Vasco, sucking down a couple of Fiestas. He hadn't had a respite since getting to Miami Beach; on his bedside table, the sealed bottle of Bacardí stared back at him. He was beginning to see it more as a trophy he would enjoy drop by drop, with lemon and ice, the way he liked, with a taste of revelry and debauchery, for when he unraveled the Lizárraga case.

He was anxious to get back home, to Little Havana, where one afternoon, as he left the hostel to cross the road, the thick thighs and meaty hips of the girl selling flowers to an elderly couple across the way at the Las Lilas flower shop transfixed him mid-stride. He waited for the couple to leave, before going in under the pretext of looking for sunflowers, tulips, orchids, some shit before asking, "I'm sorry, what's your name? Mariolys? Thanks."

The phone rang, interrupting the pleasant memory and moment of peace. Romero. Lechuga had a clean record, nothing on him. The only thing was that some time ago, the police got called to Zeke's for a complaint about some kids running a card game there. Betting. Poker to be precise. Apparently, it had started as a small group of friends that got bigger and friends stopped being friends. Officer Pérez and his men got involved. It never turned into anything, no arrests were made, warnings were given with the strict nod that it stopped right away.

"Zeke's was a beer bar, right? No liquor?"

"That's right Comanche, on Lincoln Road."

"Good Romero, got it."

11.

Joe's at the Venetian was an Irish pub, dark wooden panels on the wall, green finishes peppering the décor, and a huge pyramid of glass at the bar, built with bottles of Absolut, Stolichnaya, Johnny Walker, Bacardi. Sepia-toned photographs of Biscayne Bay and Miami Beach hung on the walls, red neon lights shone above while the speakers spat out Radiohead's "Creep." Comanche asked the bartender for the manager and not long after, a man appeared with a long white beard and locks to match, wearing a black silk robe and chocolate-colored espadrilles. He introduced himself as Roy Morris, putting himself at Comanche's service.

Comanche showed him his PI license and photos of Lizárraga.

"Recognize him?"

Of course, Morris recognized him. "The writer, why you ask?"

"He's dead Mr. Morris. The writer, Gregorio Lizárraga died a couple steps from the front door of your bar, sometime between last Saturday night and early Sunday morning. He was killed, to be more precise."

"Holy shit! That can't be, we sat there and chatted Saturday," pointing to the bar. "Caroline, two Macallans on the rocks," and turning to Comanche, "That okay?"

"Yes."

"Let's have a seat, please, tell me everything," Morris said as they took a stool at the bar.

"Better you tell me, Mr. Morris, I need to reconstruct Lizárraga's last night alive," taking a swig of the whiskey. "Lizárraga left this bar and was killed, as I said, nearby – there's a strong possibility the killer walked out of here with him."

Lizárraga had gotten there around 10:30 or 11, with Luigi Lechuga, who was kitchen staff at the bar. They were friends and drank a beer before Lechuga's shift. Lizárraga sat at the bar alone, his notebook open in front of him, and that's when Morris approached him. Lizárraga told him a local publisher was interested in his novel and he was celebrating the news. That was it. It was a busy Saturday night and Morris had to keep an eye on the business. Lizárraga remained alone, as he'd done many times before. Every now and then a familiar face would stop and say hi but nothing else. Lizárraga wasn't the big group type and seemed to enjoy his time alone. He was a watcher and was constantly scribbling down notes.

"Was this one of those familiar faces?" asked Comanche, showing Morris a photo of Runcho on his phone.

"No."

"You don't recognize this guy?"

"No, I've never seen him. Did someone say he was a patron here?"

"Nah, just asking."

"Look, Detective, this is a neighborhood bar, almost all of my clients know each other," Morris said as he pulled out a pack of Camels from his pocket, lighting one up. "I'm no one to tell you what I'm thinking, and you also haven't asked for my opinion, but I doubt the writer had any beef with anyone in here. We've never had a fight in here and more than once we've left a tab open for clients who've gotten so skunked they've left without paying, knowing they'll be by the following morning to pay their debt."

"Okay, let's say that nothing out of the ordinary happened Saturday night."

"Right, nothing out of the ordinary."

"And Luigi Lechuga?"

"No worries there, good worker. What's up with him?"

"What time did he leave that night?"

"I imagine around 3, as usual."

"You saw him, Mr. Morris? You saw him leave?"

"Well… no, not really."

"I'm gonna have to take a look at your cameras, if you don't mind," pulling the warrant out of his pocket.

Comanche followed Roy Morris' chocolate espadrilles down a poorly lit hallway and up a small spiral staircase to a second floor and into a little office that had a weathered plaque that read 'Manager' on its door.

"Make yourself at home," Morris said.

The office was messy, the desk covered with papers in no seeming order, a half drunk can of Coke Zero, another smashed down, a laptop, a desk chair, and on the floor, rolled out, a blue exercise mat under a pair of ten-pound dumbbells on which Morris did his daily stretches before work. That's why he was still in that ridiculous silk robe, he hadn't had the chance to change when Comanche arrived looking for him. Morris pulled up Saturday's recording on the laptop and hit play.

"Can you move that closer to me?" Comanche asked.

"Sure, no problem, here."

"Let me hold the mouse."

As described, the recording showed Lizárraga with Luigi Lechuga, the brief exchange with Morris, the small talk greetings with locals... and "Who's this saying hi to Lizárraga?" Comanche asked Morris, motioning to the screen. Banking executive, resident of the nearby Venetian Towers. "And this woman? She's fit." That's a spinning instructor who works at the Venetian Gym. Comanche zoomed in on the moments before Lizárraga left the bar, studying each frame carefully. He rewound, fast-forwarded, paused, changed angles, tinkered with the focus settings the software provided. He went through this about three different times, each time showed the same thing: Lizárraga saying bye to the bartender and walking out of the bar, alone. The outside cameras showed, at least to the vanishing point that Comanche could make out, Lizárraga walking alone. He went back to the interior recording, this time pausing on each person inside the bar during Lizárraga's stay in there. Comanche thought he recognized Runcho and paused. The man was wearing a Yankees hat, but the neon lights and the poor quality of the recording kept him in doubt. Morris noted, while stroking his chin, that he didn't recognize the man either. Comanche would need a copy of the recordings for Pérez's specialist to examine, hoping the department's better tech would help clean up the man's likeness for an ID. Morris, without complaint, downloaded the files into a USB and gave it to him.

"Thanks," Comanche said.

"No prob, can I offer you another whiskey?"

"I'll take a rum, if it's not too much trouble."

"None at all, glad to," said Morris as he got up to lead Comanche out the door. "You're a rum drinker?"

"Lechuga's black eye," cut in Comanche, ignoring the question and Morris' attempt at small talk. "Doesn't it seem like a bit of a coincidence that Lizárraga dies from a blow and Luigi Lechuga suddenly turns up with an eye like that?"

"Listen man, some things don't concern me so I'm not in the habit of getting into people's business."

"What do you mean?"

Luigi was a gambler. Good kid, proper, well read, loved reading, that was his chief virtue, but he had a weakness for gambling. More than once, some dudes in a blue, dark-tinted Mitsubishi with a loud muffler had come by the bar, looking to rough up Lechuga for lack of payment. Morris had to ask him to keep that shit away from the business, didn't want to see them again in his bar, not the kind of people he wanted in there. If not, he'd have to let him go. When he saw Lechuga come in that Monday, he knew it was the Mitsubishi guys who'd done it, and Lechuga told him as much.

"You say Lechuga walked in like that on Monday?"

"Yes, sir."

"He didn't work Sunday night?"

"He did, but that happened Monday morning, that's why I don't think you're right about him."

Comanche sat at the bar and Roy Morris instructed one of the waitresses to make sure his glass remained full of Bacardí, Coca-Cola, and lime. Three fingers of Bacardí, half a lime, and ice to the top like Comanche asked. The speakers at Joe's at the Venetian now blared The Cure's "Pictures of You" and he had to step outside for a sec, light up a Marlboro, and see if he could get his ideas in order.

12.

Later that night, for the first time ever, Comanche had a full view of the buildings lining up Biscayne Bay from the Venetian Causeway, the same idyllic panorama hawked on touristy postcards in souvenir shops along Ocean Drive. It was an imposing view, he had to admit, and the stars seemed to pierce the sky like fine pinpricks, and the purplish halos wafting from his cigarette followed their path until they disappeared into the night.

He gave Officer Pérez the USB and was convinced that Yankee hat was that son of a bitch Runcho, although he'd still wait for the forensics report Romero owed him. The recent intel on Lechuga changed his hypothesis regarding a scuffle with Lizárraga but the news on his gambling problem would have to be investigated. That business at Zeke's, minor as it first seemed, was looking a little different now that Morris' story was rattling in his mind. He had to consider that Lizárraga had on his monthly tally, a debt no one had been able to explain yet, could it be possible the friends shared this addiction along with their literary leanings? What if Lizárraga was knee-deep in debt and that's what the $800 was about? What if the friendship came not from their love of books, but from card games instead? He considered this, flicking his half-smoked cigarette away before going back towards the bar, Joe's at the Venetian.

It was near midnight and Lechuga would be working. Comanche picked up his pace, this was the perfect moment to face Lechuga since he knew parts of this story that no one else would.

He avoided a pair of couples who were standing outside the front door smoking, knocking into Roy Morris as he entered. He had changed into hip-hugger, boot-cut jeans, white button down with rolled-up sleeves. "Where the fuck is Lechuga?" Morris pointed the way to the kitchen. Comanche's hurry didn't give him time to ask, he just followed him as Comanche pushed his way through the crowd dancing to the Mancunian outfit James' 1993 song "Laid," echoes of the lyrics 'she only comes when she's on top' dying as he burst into the kitchen.

"Lechuga!" he screamed under the glare of a bare bulb that hung from the ceiling, casting a pale light. "Stop what you're doing and come with me, we gotta talk."

Lechuga threw the dirty fryer basket that he had in his hand, remnants of chicken wings and batter stuck in its grid, at Comanche and made a run for the emergency exit. Comanche barely avoided the greasy missile, managing to duck before bolting after Lechuga to the amazement of the kitchen staff, pulling the Glock from the waistband of his Levi's. Outside, they were met by an alleyway full of trash containers, boxes stacked against backrooms, and delivery bicycles chained to posts. Luigi Lechuga had managed a few yards of distance ahead of Comanche, who was screaming for the son of a bitch to stop. Turning at the corner, Lechuga lost his footing, but he was able to regain balance. That gave Comanche enough time to pounce on him, dropping the Glock, and connecting square on Lechuga's cheek. He didn't back down; fucker had some fight in him and landed a punch on Comanche's jaw. They wrestled to the ground, Lechuga managing to put him in a choke. But Comanche felt his way with his free hand down to Lechuga's balls and squeezed while biting down on one of his nipples. They were flopping around the floor. Comanche managed to mount him, locking Lechuga's legs beneath his, before unleashing a series of knucklers on his nose, mouth, and temples.

"Stop, shit!" Lechuga screamed through each blow, blood streaming down his face. "It was a fucking accident you son of a bitch!"

"Now you can talk, you piece of shit?" asked Comanche without stopping his barrage on Lechuga's face.

"Stop, stop, please stop! It was an accident! I didn't want to do it!"

Comanche got pulled up by his shirt, from the back, and got hooked under his arms. It was a pair of uniforms. Roy Morris had called the cops. They'd pulled up, breaking on a dime next to their brawl, the blue and red lights bouncing on the walls of buildings. They walked him into one of the squad cars and carried Lechuga's limp body into another.

13.

The hours went by slower inside the Miami Beach PD station, never-ending almost, until Officer Pérez dropped him off at El Bikini where he immediately served himself a tall Fiesta, downing it before falling into the pillow's suffocating embrace and quiet sleep that Romero interrupted with a call. Great work, he could take the day off, the following too if he liked. After clearing his mind under a warm shower, Comanche sat at the edge of the bed, the wet towel wrapped around his waist, inhaling the aroma of the Bustelo he had set to brew before showering. He would stay on the Beach, take advantage of the day off Romero had given him, and call Mariolys from the flower shop to invite her out to lunch at La Carreta the following day.

"Yooo, when are you going to check out?" Skinny asked at the front desk.

"Tomorrow, early," replied Comanche.

Before stopping at El Ilusiones, to return the Glock to Consorte and pick up the copies of *Revólver*, eat some peppery fried eggs, and spend some time without having to worry about time on the pool table's green, beaten felt, he stopped by Karina's. He found her cleaning the efficiency, broom in hand, a yellow rag, cut from what had once been a t-shirt, on her shoulder. She offered him coffee.

"I just had one, but you know what, why not?" he said, sitting at the little table with the red chairs that had now become very familiar to him.

They had caught Lizárraga's killer the night before. It was some guy, sort of friends with Lizárraga. "Lechuga, Luigi Lechuga, you know him?" She didn't. Worked at Joe's at the

Venetian, a part of Lizárraga's literary circle. It was more of an accident than a premeditated murder, Lechuga needed cash because he was a gambler and was deep in debt without a cent to his name. The people he owed money to had put a knife to his neck, pay up, or else.

He asked Lizárraga for the money, the $800 marked with a bolded "X" on his board. He must've said yes to his friend, then changed his mind, noticing he'd be in a bind himself, and at some point, between Saturday night and Sunday morning they fought. Lechuga must've taken his wallet after the scuffle, and seeing what had happened, panicked, throwing Lizárraga's phone into water to hide the evidence since they'd exchanged texts on the matter during the week.

"Son of a bitch!" Karina said, striking the surface of the small table with a tightly clenched fist. "It was an accident? An accident? That's it? This guy's not going to pay for it?"

"No, of course he will. He'll get some years in the clink. It was an accident, not premeditated murder, like

I said, but there was violence involved and it wasn't self-defense."

"Strange though, that he wouldn't leave town after killing him."

"Probably due to the guys he owed money to," said Comanche, tilting towards the coffee mug and its pleasant smell, enjoying it while the drink cooled down. "They shook him down twenty-four-seven, so he wouldn't try that shit. They'd wait for him outside his job and house."

"How much time do you think he'll get?"

"Could be between ten and fifteen years, I suppose."

"And Runcho? What do you know of Runcho?"

Nothing. Runcho was still in the wind, but they were looking for him. Every squad car on the Beach had his photo and "Wanted" flyers had gone up on storefront windows. Apparently, someone had already called in a tip, saying they'd seen him eating breakfast at an Italian spot on Española Way and Washington Avenue. He didn't remember the name of the restaurant, but when Pérez and his men got there, the lone busboy on shift did not recognize Runcho from the photo they showed him. In any case, he added with zero urgency, casting his gaze across the empty restaurant, that person wasn't there.

"Café Piccolo on Española," Karina said, a slightly raised timbre in her voice. "It was him, it had to be. He always went there for croissants."

What they couldn't figure out between them, was why Runcho had been in Lizárraga's efficiency the night that Comanche got knocked down; they would have to keep working on that. For now, though, a patrol car kept watch outside of her place.

"Did you find a place to go?" he asked.

"My friend Kina, she's letting me crash on her couch."

"Good, that's better."

"And I got the job at Al Capone, I start tonight!"

"That's good too, congrats."

There was a short, but not uncomfortable pause. Comanche

tapped out a little drum beat on the table, finished what was left of the coffee, and got up from the red chair.

He'd be on his way.

"Thanks for everything, Detective," she said, standing up and stretching out her hand.

"And you, for helping me out," shaking her hand.

"Will someone tell his ex-wife? As a courtesy maybe?"

Comanche shrugged his shoulders, he hadn't thought about that, but he'd mention it to Officer Pérez. Outside the door, after saying goodbye, he lit a Marlboro, put his black aviator Ray Bans on, and headed to El Ilusiones.

By Wild Cat

The Savage Detective

In the eighties, Miami enjoyed the notoriety of becoming a global crime capital, and from the crime beat in the editorial offices of the Herald, one reporter took it upon herself to uncover and document it all.

On July 11, 1979, around 2:30 in the afternoon, a truck burst into the parking lot of Dadeland Mall, the busiest shopping center in Miami at the time. Armed men got out and opened fire on Crown Liquors. The aftermath included injuries, bullet casings, blood on the asphalt, shattered glass, perforated car bodies, and the lives of Germán Jiménez Panesso and Juan Carlos Hernández. The first, a Colombian, was a drug trafficking kingpin, and the second, his bodyguard. The attack was a vendetta, part of the Cocaine Cowboys War, attributed to the Black Widow, Griselda Blanco, a Colombian also known as **La Madrina**. The year, 1979, is engraved in Miami's DNA due to its violence, recording 360 crimes—1980 and 1981 would record 569 and 622 respectively—and the events that most marked the city were the Dadeland Mall massacre, and later, in December, the murder of the African American Arthur McDuffie in Overtown, due to a beating by more than half a dozen police officers, without any justifiable cause. These were the wild years of Miami, but they were also years when, in the newsrooms of the press, coffee cups steamed late into the night, among them, that of Edna Buchanan at **The Miami Herald**.

Edna Buchanan was born and raised in Paterson, New Jersey. At a very young age, she showed interest in creative writing, and although she took workshops, the need to help her mother at home led her life in other directions. At 12, she began her working journey in a coat factory, then behind the counter at Woolworth's department stores, in a baby clothes shop, and a photo studio. The possibility of studying for a career was never contemplated after graduating high school.

In the summer of 1961, Edna Buchanan and her mother traveled to Miami for vacation, and it didn't take long for Edna to realize that Miami Beach would be her new home. Here, she sought a creative writing workshop, and almost unintentionally, it led to a job as a columnist at the **Miami Beach Daily Sun**, where she wrote about local news for five years. However, her professional breakthrough came at **The Miami Herald**, where, despite fighting against the editors' machismo that initially relegated her to minor cases, she managed to cover 5,000 crimes over 16 years, 3,000 of which were murders. Buchanan's work was more detective-like than journalistic.

After two failed marriages, with only a cat waiting for her to dine, she spent hours engrossed in the newsroom, the morgue, police stations, and crime scenes, gathering pieces to write a story that would appear on the front page. She always maintained the difference between her work and any other journalists was that in hers, the reader would encounter the narration of a great story. For better or worse, Edna Buchanan set the tone in many of her cases; she was the one who followed the owner of the Dadeland Mall truck to his doorstep or even changed their course, as in the McDuffie case, whose first version of events reported by the police indicated it was a motorcycle accident, but thanks to her investigation, Buchanan revealed it was due to a brutal beating by Anglo police officers against an African American.

Edna Buchanan received the Pulitzer Prize for her investigations in 1986, and that same year, a profile of her was published in **The New Yorker**, titled "Covering the Cops," written by Calvin Trillin, which said that the most talked-about people in Miami were Fidel Castro and her. By the end of that decade, she retired to follow the visceral drive to write books, and to date, she is the author of about 20 fiction and non-fiction titles and the creator of the Britt Montero series, an emblematic character in local literature, a crime reporter for a very important Miami newspaper.

Revólver Ediciones is a publication by undocumented writers and journalists clandestinely operating within Miami Beach.

COCAINE COWBOYS WANNABE

1.

"Comanche!" greeted Officer Pérez, arms crossed and slouched against his patrol car.

"Officer Pérez," replied Comanche, surprised to find him framed so by El Bikini's doors, as he walked, small suitcase in hand, wearing his black Ray-Ban aviators. He was headed to the bus stop, jonesing to return to his home in Little Havana.

"Spare me a few minutes?"

"I'm short on time, bus rolls up in seven minutes."

"I spoke with Romero; he told me you were leaving."

"That's right."

"Stay on a couple days."

"Not possible," Comanche thought about his unfinished business with Romero and Mariolys, whom, so far, he had only been able to woo with cortaditos made with evaporated milk from the little window next to the flower shop. But he had her on the line for a hearty *carne con papa* lunch at La Carreta.

"It's about Runcho," Pérez insisted. "Give me 15, maybe 20 minutes, and if it doesn't tickle you, I'll have one of my guys drive you to Little Havana."

Juan Guerra, aka Da Vinci, one of the Flamingo Park dealers, had died under suspicious circumstances. Da Vinci lived at the Mirador, on West Avenue, and the concierge had called the cops because the neighbors were complaining about the loud music blasting from his apartment. He and the neighbors had banged on his door to no avail. Finally, Officer Pérez and his men picked the lock and went in. Dalida's "Ciao Amore, Ciao," was turned all the way up and on repeat. Da Vinci was laid out on the cold, white marble floor. He had a small, leopard print skirt on, no underwear, freshly shaved legs, and an electric blue wig. Just off to his side, a sports bag filled with little coke-filled Ziplocs. The autopsy revealed a massive heart attack, brought on by acute cocaine toxicity and alcohol, vodka to be precise, a combo that in excess, taxed his heart beyond its natural capabilities. The forensic team found Runcho's fingerprints on Da Vinci's body, the marble, the empty Stolichnaya bottle, next to the hi-fi, on the grapefruit rinds on the rim of the glasses, the fridge, and the sports bag. Da Vinci had traces of semen in his rectum, and though there was no DNA test, his buttocks and hips were covered in Runcho's fingerprints. It wasn't hard to figure out who'd mounted him.

"So… Runcho's quite a hoe," said Comanche, lighting up a Marlboro and letting out a long plume of smoke.

"That's not what's interesting," said Pérez.

With the accusations of violence and sexual battery this guy was dragging on about, on top of possession and weed, now with this, the list got longer. Plus, if Comanche wanted to press charges for battery due to the haymaker he'd eaten at Lizárraga's efficiency, he could. The case had gotten big enough already for Pérez to put a task force on it.

"Okay," agreed Comanche. "If Runcho's still lurking around here, okay, I'll stay. And add my charge to it, count on it."

"He didn't flee like we suspected; he's hiding."

"What's the name of the café on Española and Washington? Remember it?"

"El Piccolo, yeah, why?"

"I've been told he's a regular for breakfast there."

"Interesting," said Pérez. "Especially since the waiter said he didn't recognize his face."

"Might be good to have eyes on the joint," Comanche suggested. "Is Da Vinci's apartment open for a look?"

"Sure, I'll let my guys know," said Pérez. "We have it blocked but they can let you in if it's necessary."

"Hmm, maybe not. What about the bag with the drugs?"

"At the station, in evidence, but I have something for you," Pérez said as he opened his patrol car's door, reaching for the glove compartment. "Everything inside is yours," he said as he handed Comanche an envelope. "Photos from the crime scene and plenty of cash for your incidentals. Pair of coke baggies too."

Comanche flicked away his Marlboro, took off his aviators, hanging them on his shirt collar. Looking at the contents of the envelope, "What if I need more cash?"

"I doubt you will, but if you do, just let me know."

Comanche put his glasses back on and shook Pérez's hand.

He'd had a hard time getting out of bed that morning because he had finally gotten around to that bottle of Bacardí, ending up sprawled out on the mattress in his underwear. It had been when he was about to make his third fiesta that he noticed the ice, previously held in a McDonald's cup, had turned to water, and Skinny was no longer at the front desk to get him some from the kitchen. Not thrilled, but also not really burdened by this, he made his way to the Al Capone, where Karina would be debuting behind the bar, the violet neon lights hanging from the ceiling made Capone's caricature profile on the wall pop, and the music welcomed Comanche in a warm embrace. Everything got better when he went to the bathroom and swapped a pair of twenties for a baggie of that magical dust that traveled on the expressway of his nose into his brain, filling his whole body with adrenaline.

He texted Mariolys, to excuse himself because the job had been extended and they'd need him a few more days. He stood under the warm water in the shower – completely lathered with mentholated suds, trickling down his face, chest, neck, stomach, his balls – he had to wash the night off of him, afterwards, his neurons and his body would feel better. A lot better.

2.

"Where have you been?" barked Romero. "I've called you a thousand times."

"I'm at El Bikini, I just woke up... just saw your missed calls..."

"What do you mean 'at El Bikini?' I've been waiting for you here since 10 a.m. and now it's well after 3!"

"I'm not following..."

"The fuck you're not Comanche! I bet you got torn up last night and you're just opening your eyes now!"

"Wait a minute, Romero, wait a minute." Comanche backtracked his day. Officer Pérez caught him on the way out of El Bikini and asked him to stay on Runcho and his

Flamingo Park gang case. Pérez had told him he'd told Romero about it and that it was okay.

"That's a fucking lie, asshole. I'm finding that out now, from you!"

"Well, Pérez is a son of a bitch," Comanche said. He would grab his things and leave right away. But Romero told him not to, to stay put. After all, if Officer Pérez asked him, it was because he needed him, and it wouldn't be wise to get on his bad side. He would call the officer right away to let him know Comanche would stay on and offer his assistance. Comanche didn't care for that quick about-face from Romero, it was cowardly, submissive.

"But tell me a little more before I call him," asked Romero.

"Yeah well, you can ask him," said Comanche as he hung up.

After brushing his teeth and getting dressed, he checked his messages, one was from Mariolys, from earlier in the day, that it was shame they wouldn't see each other, she'd been looking forward to their lunch date. The other one was a new one, from Romero, urging him to call him back.

"Comanche."

"What's up?"

"This case is serious."

Flamingo Park was a family space and the epicenter of South Beach's tennis community, but it had been overrun by drugs and thugs. The straw that broke the camel's back a few months ago and triggered the investigation was when, one afternoon during the Miami Beach Chamber of Commerce tennis tournament, Runcho mistakenly thought one of the players, a high-ranking executive of the Chamber, had come to buy coke from him. He approached him, showed him a baggie, and asked for money. Realizing he'd messed up, he took off running and disappeared for a few days until things cooled down. The executive immediately made a couple of calls, pulled some strings, and since then, Runcho had been on their radar, but they never had enough personnel or time to fully focus on it. The streets of Miami Beach were a pressure cooker, with their resources being drained by the daily shootings and stabbings. Pérez needed Comanche; he had to handle this case on the down-low without drawing media attention. The beach was packed with tourists, and they couldn't afford to scare them off with a media circus.

3.

The bright yellow balls bounced back and forth across two courts in Flamingo Park. The rest of the courts were empty, and the carefree laughter of children and their mothers came from the swings in the playground. Comanche walked the expanse of the park, looking at everything and deemed it a futile exercise. He headed to a little white house, the park's tennis kiosk for reservations. It was simple: a gabled roof with wooden beams and decorated with racquets in various stages of decay and posters of Pete Sampras, Andre Agassi, Serena Williams.

"Hi friend, how can I help you?" asked the clerk at the counter, sitting next to a Gatorade vending machine. "Need a court later today?"

"I'm looking for Runcho."

"Excuse me? Who?"

"Runcho."

"No, I don't know who that is," he said as he lowered his gaze onto the reservation's notebook in front of him.

"Listen, brother," said Comanche as he pulled his Ray-Bans off, hanging them from his collar as he slapped his PI ID on the counter. "You better talk, I don't like to get jerked around."

"Hey man, hey! I don't know what this is, but I don't like it…"

"And you'll like it even less if you don't talk." Comanche took Runcho's photos from his pocket and threw them on the counter. "Here he is, in case you forgot what his face looks like. I'm looking for this fucker and his friends because they've been dealing dope in YOUR park, under YOUR nose, and if you don't start talking, I'll drag your ass down to the station and hold you there until your memory starts working again."

The clerk put his hands up, trembling, he had nothing

to do with those guys. He'd swear to that. They'd cornered him inside the kiosk a long time ago – Runcho, Da Vinci, and Fiorito – and told him that if he valued his life, he'd stay out of their business. One of them, Fiorito, had a gun, a big gun. All they wanted was simple, be quiet and let them do their thing.

"I don't believe a fucking word. You're part of the gang too and you're going down."

The clerk said nothing, only lowered his gaze even more.

"Why didn't you call the cops?"

"I don't have papers, man, and I didn't want to get into it with them too. Especially after seeing Fiorito's gun."

"Tell me something I don't know then," demanded Comanche. "I doubt you only know as much as I already know after all this time sharing the park with them."

He insisted, again, that he had nothing else to say, that he didn't know anything else about them, and that he had nothing to do with them – even that one time he bumped into them at Joe's on the Venetian – they had ignored him when he tried to say hello. The closest he came to exchanging pleasantries was when he found himself face-to-face with Runcho in one of the bar's hallways, and the thug grabbed him by the arm, forcing it up a bit, and told him that hellos were only from far away if they had to be, and away from the tennis courts he better not act like he knew them. If he wanted to keep on living.

"Joe's at the Venetian?" interrupted Comanche.

"Yes."

"When was that?"

The clerk paused. He was visibly going over dates in his mind. "Maybe less than a year ago?" The Hemingway Bar was still open, he remembered that because he and his friends debated going there or Joe's. The Hemingway had closed about a year ago. That didn't mean that Joe's at the Venetian was the bar Runcho frequented. Shit, on South Beach there was a bar on every corner. Maybe it was a coincidence, but

Joe's kept ringing in his ear. Apparently, that was all the clerk knew or could tell about the gang beyond the confines of Flamingo Park.

"What's your name?" Comanche asked.

"Steve Caballero."

"Okay, Steve Caballero. I'll take your word for it."

4.

Comanche sat on one of Flamingo Park's benches facing Meridian Avenue, sucking on a Marlboro while he thought of his next steps. Too much of a coincidence that Steve Caballero had seen Runcho at Joe's, as he had when he looked at the camera footage with Roy Morris. Roy Morris who had assured him that he knew everyone at his bar but not this kid who didn't frequent it. Two coincidences were too much. Joe's had to be Runcho's watering hole, he had to figure that out, and Morris was either lying or hiding something. He was deep in thought trying to figure that out when he felt a hand on his shoulder. It was Karina. She was going home from a mass Cabalito, La Chismosa's manager, had organized in honor of Lizárraga at the church on Washington and 5th. She thought it was weird to find him there, that he'd gone back home to Little Havana already. He told her the case had taken a turn, not because of Lizárraga's death, but because of Runcho, but he didn't offer up any more details other than Runcho was not on the run but hiding, somewhere nearby, and he was after him and his gang.

"Wanna tell me more over a coffee?" She offered while explaining that she wasn't meddling into his business but because she was afraid of Runcho. "I've been staying with my friend Kina, but we can cross the street to my apartment so we can talk."

"That would be great," he said, flicking his butt away. "Your friend Kina lives nearby?"

"A little further down, between Española and Drexel."

"I liked that bar you're working at."

"Oh yeah," she said. "It's hot right now. The live music

is the biggest draw. We've got Pistolas Rosadas booked and everyone's going crazy over their singer, La Chica más pop de South Beach. Al Capone and Joe's are the hot bars now."

"Huh. The famous Joe's on the Venetian."

"Famous how?" she asked, opening the door to her efficiency. "After you, Inspector."

"It keeps coming up," said Comanche, sitting yet again on one of the little red chairs that he'd become so familiar with by now. He hadn't known about Lizárraga's mass.

She herself had been told at the last minute. It was a small affair, simple. Cabalito was a devout Catholic, not her, but Cabalito didn't miss a Sunday at church; the priest knew him and organized the ceremony, the prayers and supplications for Lizárraga. The guys from the taqueria were there, as were the guys from *Revólver*, herself, and an old coworker of Lizárraga's from Bella Napolitana, the joint he worked at when he first got here. Perú, that's what Lizárraga called him, they were pretty good friends, even from before Lizárraga took up writing, back when he was just an avid reader.

Perú knew the story behind Lizárraga and his wife, the tragedy. Facundo, their boy, had fainted one Sunday, playing soccer with friends. They took him to the ER. "It's probably because he's a little weak, compared to the other boys…" his wife, Estela, had repeated over and over, as they waited their turn, slowly chewing the beef empanada Lizárraga had bought in the hospital's cafeteria. It had been a few days, and she hadn't eaten well.

"Facundo Lizárraga?" asked a nurse, decked in blue scrubs that looked like a clear pool in summertime, masked, stethoscope hanging, his gaze wandering over the chilly little room with smoky-colored tiles and dim light.

"Here," said Estela, taking Facundo by the hand. Lizárraga followed.

X-rays, encephalograms, and a couple vials of Facundo's blood. At first glance, it didn't look like anything serious.

"You have to eat your food, Facundo," Estela scolded the boy. In any case, the nurse explained the doctor would review the results closely. If anything came up, they'd call them.

The phone rang in their modest home a few days later, mid-morning. Estela was making mashed potatoes and crispy, thin beef *milanesas*.

"Is this Mrs. Estela Lizárraga?"

"Speaking," she said, balancing the receiver between her shoulder and her cheek as she wiped away the breadcrumbs and egg whites on her Porky Pig apron.

"We're calling from Dr. Anselmo Franceschini's office."

Franceschini himself came out to greet them and usher them into his office. He wore an immaculate white robe, his name stitched in blue cursive lettering. He gave the boy a pair of Transformers to play with in the lobby. They sat in the office, across from Franceschini's desk, with an open case file folder containing photos that looked like a pumpkin and the results of blood tests: band cells, white blood cells, glucose levels. "You follow me so far?" Lizárraga nodded, as did Estela. Then the doctor focused on the photos. They were of the boy's brain. A small mass, a tiny little ball, had grown there, which he circled with his pen. It had been there for at least three months, at the top, and it would keep growing. Lizárraga couldn't bring himself to look at Estela; his eyes kept shifting between the pumpkin, the tiny, tiny, insignificant little ball, and Franceschini's gold Cross pen, which was drawing lines and dots that connected to form letters and words: tumor, cancer, life expectancy. From the lobby the boy cried, "Mom? Dad? Can we go now?"

Lizárraga had only come to Miami for work, alone, so he could pay for the treatments from here. His wife and kid had stayed behind in Argentina, and when Facundo died, Lizárraga decided he never wanted to return to his country, and his wife, Estela, refused to move from their home in Buenos Aires near Retiro on the northeast end of the city. And even less to move to the United States. To do what?

Fucking Yankees. Facundo's death ended their marriage. Perú was inconsolable, it had been some time since they'd seen each other, because of work, shitty hours, but they would chat on the phone any time there was a Champions League match or to recommend each other books or to hear Lizárraga update him on *Ciudad Maldita*. He had read the manuscript early on, ahead of anyone else and had made some suggestions to him. What Perú knew about books and literature was thanks to Lizárraga.

"Black, no milk, no sugar, right?" asked Karina, leaving the steaming cup of coffee on the table in front of him.

"Yes," he said, lighting up a Marlboro.

They had found Da Vinci dead in his apartment, from a cocaine overdose and a massive heart attack, under strange circumstances: sex, alcohol, drugs, and the police seized a briefcase full of drugs, which they believed was being trafficked at Flamingo Park. Runcho was deeply implicated, his fingerprints were everywhere, even on Da Vinci's body.

"I'll never understand that son of a bitch," she said.

Comanche looked at the time on his phone, he had to go, it was as good a time as any to pay Roy Morris a visit before the bar got busy. Karina was on her way for a run at South Pointe Park, on the end of the island.

"How long will you be around?"

"As long as this case takes, I guess."

"Come by my bar, I'm on shift every night this week."

Comanche thanked her for the coffee, putting his aviators on at the door. At that time in the afternoon, the dying sunlight shone brighter, making it impossible for him to see without them.

5.

The bar at Joe's on the Venetian had only one person, a man staring blankly into the foam of his beer. In the background, Madonna was singing "La Isla Bonita" at a moderate volume.

"Welcome back," said Caroline, the bartender, as she dried glasses with a white cloth.

"Roy Morris is in his office, right?" asked Comanche, giving the place a quick glance, confirming that he wasn't around.

He didn't wait for an answer, assuming Morris was in his office, and headed for the spiral staircase leading up to it. The door was open, and Morris, dressed in his black silk robe and espadrilles, was updating an Excel sheet with the inventory figures for Absolut, Stolichnaya, Johnnie Walker, Macallan, Bacardi, and Zacapa bottles. Comanche barged in, unannounced, startling Morris, who hadn't expected him to come back so soon. As he stood up to offer a handshake, he received a kick to the chest, ending up on the floor with Comanche on top of him: "You're a fucking bastard, you lied, you fucking bastard!" He had little patience and less time. He got up and ordered Morris back to his chair. Even though he had shown him photos of Runcho the night before Lechuga's arrest, he put more photos of Runcho on the desk. He needed to find him; he knew Runcho was a regular at the bar, and if Morris didn't want to come clean, a squad car would take him to the Miami Beach Police Department's interrogation room.

"Can we close the door to talk more privately?" Morris asked, still recovering and rubbing his chest.

"You stay where you are," said Comanche, walking to the

door, his eyes fixed on Morris. "I'm listening, talk. Talk, damn it."

Morris didn't want trouble in his bar, which had been iconic since the Eighties when he was just coming of age and had his first drinks at the bar, then run by Jane, a redhead who balanced the job while studying law at the University of Miami. Every Thursday, her classmates were the main attraction at Ladies' Night. They made the place famous. Some even preferred it to the Mutiny Hotel across the bay in Coconut Grove. When the previous owners, an Irish couple who were ready to spend their final years in Dublin, handed the business over to Morris, one of the conditions was to maintain its tradition and prestige. He emphasized this as he glanced at the wall, where photos of journalists, editors, and writers from *The Miami Herald* and some celebrities who were regulars hung. That's why he had given information about Lechuga and the bettors, it created a bad atmosphere. He helped and collaborated with Comanche in every way he could. Maybe, and he admitted this, he made a mistake denying that he knew Runcho.

Runcho was indeed a regular at Joe's, and Morris knew he sold coke. He had no proof, had never witnessed a deal, but some things are known, open secrets. Every bar has prostitutes looking for a pickup and scum who make sure noses get powdered; it's part of the logistics, the operation. So long as they didn't cause trouble, owners turned a blind eye.

"Okay, Morris," Comanche said. "I can't do anything with just the fact that you knew who he was. I want something worth my while, cuz if not, I'm calling Officer Pérez and asking him to take you in for an official interrogation. And since we already know you're a fucking liar, they're not going to treat you so nicely as I'm doing snow."

"I have nothing left to say to you, Detective," shrinking his shoulders. "Do what you gotta do. I've never even spoke with Gitano or El Runcho. Never ever."

"El Runcho and who?"

"Gitano," Morris said, clearing his throat with a sip from a small can of Coke Zero.

"Who is Gitano?"

"You don't know Gitano?"

"No and I already told you I'm short on time and patience, who the fuck is he? Talk!"

"Gitano is their boss."

"I thought Runcho was the boss," said Comanche.

Gitano rarely went by Joe's. Just occasionally to meet an unsatisfied client. He was the head, Runcho his right hand, and the rest of the bootlickers, his eyes and ears. Gitano was tall, skinny, olive-skinned, jet-black hair pulled into a ponytail, huge eyes – darker than his hair – with golden hoops hanging from his ears. He looked like a taller version of the famed Flamenco singer, Diego el Cigala.

"When's the last time you saw Gitano?"

"Maybe two or three weeks ago… but it had been ages before that."

"I'mma need you to sit with a sketch artist."

"Sure, no problem. If you want, I can check the cameras, maybe that will be better, but it'll take a couple of hours."

"How many?"

"I can spend all night sitting here looking."

"Then spend all night, sitting there. Looking."

"Whatever you say, man."

"I'm going to call in for a unit to watch your exits. That way I can be sure you won't be scurrying out of here."

"C'mon, Detective, you still don't trust me after kicking me down like Kenya Kimura?"

6.

A woman was singing onstage at Al Capone's, strumming her guitar with the gentleness of a new lover's touch. She wore a jean jacket, an Andrés Calamaro t-shirt from his album Honestidad Brutal, and black Chuck Taylors. A disco ball hung from the ceiling, refracting the violet neon light, giving her an even paler tone to her milk bone skin. She was La Chica más pop de South Beach with her band, Pistolas Rosadas. Their set was just starting, and Comanche found a spot at Karina's bar and there, standing up front and center was Wild Cat and the guys from *Revólver*.

"*Che,*" Karina said smiling. "You decided to pass by! Nice, this is just getting started."

"I gotta be up early tomorrow, can't have a repeat of last night."

"Anything new on that jerk, Runcho?"

"Nothing, so far."

"Want a beer? What can I get you?"

"Rum."

"With?"

"Coke and a lime."

Karina turned to prepare the drink, and he took in her silhouette: black pants, tight – very tight, outlining a firm ass. The gym was paying off; it wasn't big and round, something you'd smack with both hands like Mariolys', which, although he hadn't seen it yet, he imagined it to be like that, or like the ones you'd see in the aisles and corridors of the Floridita Discount Supermarket or the Navarro in Little Havana. Although he had already noticed her attributes a few days earlier in her apartment when she returned from running at South Pointe, wearing leggings, this time, that figure sent a jolt of adrenaline straight to his cock.

"Try it and tell me if it needs more lime, Coke, or ice," Karina said, placing the drink on top of a coaster bearing Capone's silhouette on the wooden bar top.

"It's good," Comanche said, smacking his lips. It wasn't one of his fiestas that he alone knew how to make and had no comparison amongst rum beverages.

"Good," she said, excusing herself to tend to a couple who'd elbowed in onto the bar and had signaled for her.

Even though he told Morris he didn't believe him, it looked like he hadn't lied. This Gitano could open some doors, but he'd need Officer Pérez to identify him, and he'd need Consorte too. The first thing he'd do the following day would be to have breakfast at Ilusiones.

One of Consorte's many functions within Miami Beach's seedy underbelly, was to serve as go-between for the dealers and the scaredy-cat cokeheads who could never muster the gall – or put themselves on the line – to score that hit that would get them through the night.

"What do you think of Pistolas?" asked Karina as she made her way back to him.

"Good," he said absently, not really wanting to say he'd paid them no mind.

"Another one?" she asked, motioning towards his glass, now a shipwrecked slice of lime floating on the melted remains of the final ice cube.

"Sure, thanks."

Comanche was about to go to the bathroom when he ran into Wild Cat, who recognized him and greeted him with hesitation. Comanche returned the greeting and told him that he had read one of his articles the day before, very good, "The Savage Detective," about a journalist from *The Miami Herald* who covered crime stories. Wild Cat appreciated the compliment; that was his Tropical Noir column, where he wrote about Miami's violence and was preparing an upcoming piece dedicated to

Lizárraga, a great connoisseur of the genre. Comanche's cell phone vibrated in his pocket. He excused himself, saying he needed to step out to take the call. Wild Cat was at a table next to the stage with the *Revólver* crew, suggesting that he passed by.

"Morris," said Comanche at the door of Al Capone's, "Didn't expect your call so soon."

"I have it, Detective. Come by whenever."

"I'm on my way."

Comanche took a Marlboro out of the pack, held it with his teeth, lit it, and sent a text to Karina, apologizing for leaving the second rum unfinished and not paying. He had to handle something urgent and would bring the money to her house. He made his way down Washington Avenue. At that hour it was a parade of king size asses, silicone mountains, shaved breasts, hair slicked back with gel, convertible cars blasting hip-hop, corners populated by prostitutes who'd blow you for 30 bucks, souvenir shop windows, tattoo studios, and pizzeria ads flashing "Open."

Comanche entered Joe's on the Venetian through the back door, the same one he had used a couple of nights ago after Luigi Lechuga. Morris was waiting for him in his office. Upon seeing him, he offered his chair in front of the computer: "All yours, Mr. Comanche. Here's Gitano in zoom." Comanche paused, advanced, rewound, and played in slow motion.

"Can I print this?" he asked, pausing on Gitano's face.

"Let me help," Morris replied, took the mouse, and clicked on the printer icon.

Comanche stood up and extended his hand. "Thank you, Morris."

"Sorry, Detective, for lying the other day," Morris apologized and put three copies of Gitano's face into a manila envelope.

"It's forgotten."

7.

Comanche didn't know of a better way to hit "play" and get his day going other than standing under a hot stream in the shower, completely lathered in mentholated suds, and plopping onto his bed, damp towel around his waist, sucking down his first Marlboro while the coffee pot shrieked on the stove, impregnating the whole place with the delicious aroma of Café Bustelo. And that's just what he did. Then he called Romero for a debrief on his latest findings, and then Pérez right after. He needed to meet with him, but his morning was already taken up with a case-related errand – though he didn't tell him where or with whom – and Pérez told him to meet him at Los Latinos at noon.

"Wassup, buddy?" greeted Skinny when Comanche passed by the front desk.

"All good, enjoy, that looks delicious," said Comanche, eyeing Skinny's McDonald's breakfast burrito.

"You hungry? Want some?"

"Nah, I'm good. Heading over to Ilusiones for a bite."

"Later, man."

Willie Colón's "Talento de TV" greeted Comanche as he entered Ilusiones, a welcome sound amongst the clang of balls crashing across the tables inside. There he was, El Chamizo, Comanche's eternal rival in the betting annals of El Ilusiones, standing behind a table. He'd never beaten Comanche, but he was always down to play, gaining invaluable experience and skills he'd then apply on his schoolmates at Miami Dade College.

"Three fried eggs with lots of pepper," said Comanche. Neither Consorte, who was thumbing through the latest issue of *Revólver*, nor El Chamizo had noticed him come in.

"Holy shit, look who it is," Chamizo said, laying the cue against the wall behind him, opening his arms to hug Comanche.

"I thought you were back in Little Havana," said Consorte, putting the magazine aside.

"Got two 20's here, bitch," said Chamizo, pulling out his wallet. "C'mon, before I lose you for a couple of months."

"Let me talk to Consorte," said Comanche. "Then I'll break your ass."

"Word, okay," Chamizo said, grabbing the cue and breaking the neat triangle of balls he'd organized on the felt.

"What's up, bro?" asked Consorte. "For real, I thought you were back home giving them Little Havana ladies the business."

"Not yet," he said, a bit dryly, as he produced the manila envelope from his pocket.

"Who are these beauties?"

One was dead, Da Vinci, and the other, Fiorito, wasn't

of interest to anyone. Putting those back in the envelope, Comanche left a pair on the counter. Gitano, the dark one with the hoops and ponytail heads a gang running coke out of Flamingo Park, and Runcho, his righthand man. The cops were looking for them, on and off, for a while now, but when Runcho got linked to Lizárraga's murder, the gang was back on the radar. A task force had been assembled and Comanche was on the case with them. But he needed help – he needed Consorte's contacts to help him find them. Runcho had vanished but his prints were all over Da Vinci's murder scene – on the body and a sports bag full of drugs – which meant he was nearby.

What Comanche was asking for wouldn't be hard to do. He'd be happy to help, as usual, even in a business where throwing him a bone or two could cost him his liberty. Or his life.

"Better lend me the piece again."

"Again?"

"Yeah, and I'll need the other thing too. I gotta figure this out."

"You're asking for too much, brother."

"If I don't come correct with Romero on a case for Officer Pérez, it's the street for me."

"Who's Romero?"

"The guy who runs the agency I work for, the fuck? I've told you a hundred times."

"You're a real jerkoff, you know? A real jerkoff that always has the last word, gets his way and shit," said Consorte, defeated. "I guess that's why you're a good detective."

"You gonna help me or what?"

"Yeah, leave me the photos and go play a round with Chamizo before I change my mind. I'll bring your eggs over."

"It's three eggs."

"Yeah, I fucking know."

"With lots of pepper."

"Bro, go to the fucking table already or you're not getting shit."

Comanche pulled a cue from the wall. He chalked the tip, patted his hand on the talc cone, and walked over to Chamizo.

"Twenty a ball," said Comanche, putting a bill into the middle pocket.

"There you go, homie, I thought we weren't gonna do this."

"Work comes first, you know how it is," said Comanche as he pulled his Marlboros out.

"I can do two, maybe three rounds, depends how long each one takes," said Chamizo, looking at his watch. "I have a class at 11."

"What are you in school for?"

"Business, over at the Miami Dade campus in Downtown."

They arranged the balls in the triangle as Comanche asked Consorte to put some Héctor Lavoe on and nodded to Chamizo to break. In turn, the young wannabe hustler forced a shot without thinking that scattered the balls all over the felt.

"Turn it up, Consorte," said Comanche, motioning upwards with his thumb.

Eh, vamos a bailar la murga

La murga de Panamá

The striped, yellow one went in. Chamizo would be stripes.

Esto es una cosa fácil

Y muy buena pa'bailar

Comanche would play solids.

Ay tú tienes un caminao

Que me tienes trastornao

Comanche walked around the table, assessing his shots,

bending over finally to focus on his shot. That beaten felt, a green horizon pockmarked by cigarette burns, transported him back to his youth when he'd run away from the yellowed walls of his house, his bedroom, away from his dad's homosexuality and the affair he'd been having with a colleague, a skinny guy with a thin mustache. A secret his mother never found out, the cancer eating her before it couldn't be hidden anymore. On Sundays at noon, around the time the referee blew the whistle to start the ninety minutes of the local soccer league match, the skinny guy with the thin mustache and his wife arrived at Comanche's house. The women would settle in the kitchen to season the tomatoes and lettuce and prepare the *arroz con leche* for later; meanwhile, the men took charge of the grill, roasting sausages, and the *morcillas*, doing whatever it took to stay right there and have that pair in the kitchen—with their sagging breasts, smelling of garlic and seasonings on their cuticles—disappear from their lives.

"Here you go," said Consorte, putting the fried eggs and buttery, toasted Cuban bread next to him. "And there on the house," placing a couple of ham croquetas next to the plates.

They went two rounds, Comanche winning both. They played a third, without betting. If Chamizo had put down what was left in his wallet, he'd be going without lunch that day. Comanche showed him how to bank the shots, use the sides effectively, tapping the cue here and there, reminding him that it wasn't about sinking the easy shot but leaving oneself better positioned for the next one. That it was just as important to block your opponent's shots too.

"C'mere bro," shouted Consorte from the bar.

Comanche left his cue on the table as Chamizo said he was leaving. He needed to grab some things from his house before class and it was well past 10.

Consorte had someone in mind to help Comanche, one of South Beach's heaviest heavies when it came to moving coke, el Papito. He'd agreed to meet Comanche after Consorte sent him Gitano and Runcho's photos in a text. Papito knew the sons of bitches and they owed him big. Consorte told Comanche that Papito had made it very clear if his name leaked from their convo, if the police even looked at him – shit, even brought him in – nothing would happen to him, wouldn't even be in holding for three hours until he bailed out. But on that same day, Consorte and Comanche would be found with the telltale gaping hole of hollow points on their foreheads.

"You're the best, Consorte."

"Easy."

"Where and when with Papito?"

"Here, at 3," Consorte said, letting Comanche know he'd close the bar so he and Papito could meet in the alleyway. Neither of them would want to come up in the Ilusiones cameras.

"How much for the eggs?" asked Comanche, lighting up a Marlboro.

"Nothing bro, you're good."

Keeping Comanche happy let Consorte do as he pleased with Papito or anyone.

"Let me get a refill," said Comanche, motioning to the empty water jug next to him.

As Consorte turned to the sliding glass fridge behind him, Comanche leafed through the *Revólver* on the counter.

"Hand me your glass," said Consorte.

"I hung with one of these guys at the Al Capone," said Comanche handing over his glass.

"Which one?"

"The guy you brought the other day, Wild Cat."

"I like his pieces."

"Yeah, I read the Savage Detective, interesting."

"The one about the lady reporter from *The Herald* who caught every crime in the 80's?"

"Yeah, that one."

"Take the magazine if you want," Consorte said. "I already finished it. Wild Cat's got a piece in there you might like."

"Oh yeah? What?"

"Scarface."

"Scarface?"

"Yup," said Consorte. "It's got the whole history of how the movie was originally a book inspired by Al Capone's bio."

"I'll grab the magazine after I talk with Papito." Comanche thought maybe there would be a clue in the magazine. It couldn't hurt to read. "I'll take it then along with the piece."

8.

The $9.99 lunch special included soup with the entrée, one of the bigger draws keeping the tables at Los Latinos full. Pérez was waiting for him in the back, next to a wall covered in weathered posters of the Aztec ruins. Comanche didn't hide his annoyance at Pérez lying about squaring away the extra time with Romero. The officer, raising his hands in a half-assed shrug flatly said it had to be that way. Specially in urgent cases like this. If they were going to work the case hand-to-hand, it would be better without a third wheel. Pérez liked that old fuck Romero, his mentor on the force before striking out to form his own agency – the one Comanche worked for – but he'd gotten too bureaucratic over the years.

He liked his old lady too, Nancy, who used to cook the best ox steak Pérez had ever tasted. Every Friday, when he and Romero finished their shift at the same time, they would find the TV at Romero's house tuned to *Miami Vice*, a table set for three, with *congrí* and baked potatoes in the center to accompany the steak, and a bottle of Marqués de Riscal, Reserva, slowly emptying in front of Sonny Crockett's linen suits and the smoke from the Cohibas.

Even though Comanche didn't like working with intermediaries either, he didn't like the explanation. Next time, he'd grab his things and leave, fuck the case.

"Do you gentlemen know what you want?" asked the waitress, notepad in hand, wearing a black t-shirt emblazoned with the slogan: Here, we're all proud Cholos!

"Give us a minute, hon," replied Pérez.

"Something to drink in the meantime?"

Pérez asked for a *manzanita* Postobón and Comanche a Coca-Cola.

She excused herself, turning towards the kitchen doors, showing the back of the t-shirt: And you? Are you a proud Cholo too?

"They've got plantain soup and either beef or chicken *vaca frita*," said Pérez. "It's on me, the beef's good."

"Cool, but don't forget what I just told you."

"Don't worry about it, we don't have to dwell on that."

Comanche took out Gitano's photo from the envelope and placed it on the table. That was the man they were looking for. El Gitano. Runcho was only his right-hand man. Comanche needed Pérez to search for his record and find absolutely everything he could; the only thing they had so far was his photo and nickname – they didn't even know his real name. Pérez took the photo, examined it closely, trying to see if he looked familiar or if he could remember or relate it to something, but nothing came to mind.

"And what do we know about Runcho?" Pérez asked. Two of his officers had breakfasted at el Piccolo, but no signs.

"Nothing, he's disappeared."

The Runcho thing seemed strange. It happened after fighting with Karina. Maybe it was logical since he hit her and might fear she would retaliate, though it wasn't the first time, and nothing happened. But then he hit Comanche on the head, at Lizárraga's efficiency, when Lizárraga was already dead. If Runcho wasn't Lizárraga's murderer, what the hell was he doing there the night Comanche went in? After that, he was never seen again, until his fingerprints showed up on Da Vinci's body and the sports bag full of drugs.

"Here are your sodas," said the waitress, holding the drinks on a red plastic tray. "Know what you want to order?"

"Two beef *vaca fritas*," Pérez ordered.

"With rice and maduros?" asked the waitress, and they both said yes.

"Who tipped you to Gitano?"

"Let's set a rule," Comanche proposed. "If you agree."

"What rule?"

"My sources stay with me."

"Fine, agreed."

"When do you think you can get me shit on Gitano?"

"Give me a few hours."

"Good. I think I'll get something else today, too."

The waitress brought their food on her red tray and set them down in front of each of them. Would they need anything else? No? Were they good? And to please let her know if they needed anything else. Comanche took a bite, very good. Pérez agreed, the *vaca frita* was delicious. He ate lunch there almost every day and sprinkled some salt on his.

"Enjoy."

"Thanks, same to you. Pass the salt?"

The meal was quick; they paid and left, as other customers were waiting. Outside, Comanche put on his aviators, lit a Marlboro, and offered one to Pérez, who declined and said goodbye, needing to head to the Police Department to continue the search for Gitano.

Comanche set off for El Bikini, but halfway there, he changed his plans and headed to Karina's instead. If she was home, he would take the opportunity to pay her the rums he owed. He knocked a couple of times. Nothing. He figured she might be at Kina's place. As he was leaving, though, he heard a voice behind him calling, "Inspector, inspector." She was half-asleep, almost didn't hear the door, wearing a blue sweater that swallowed her hands and a pair of Adidas pants several sizes too big. Karina had left the bar late the previous night, gone to Kina's, and crashed on the couch without sleeping. She had a window behind her, through which the first yellow streaks of morning filtered through, hitting her face. Every 10 minutes, she sat up and took sips from the water bottle beside her, which was next to her cell phone and the tips from her shift. Comanche pulled out a $20 bill to pay for the rums, but Karina didn't accept and invited him in, saying she was making coffee, which was starting to become a regular thing.

"Anything on Runcho?" Karina asked. "I can't take Kina's couch anymore; I need better rest; I want to come back to my place."

"No sign of Runcho," said Comanche, sitting at the table while Karina prepared the coffee, his eyes on the black thong and bra she'd left on the floor beside her unmade bed before crawling into it.

"What do you recommend?"

"If you want, come back," Comanche said, lighting a Marlboro. He no longer believed Karina's safety was at risk. Runcho was hiding because of Da Vinci's death and drugs, not her.

"Ok. Oh, yesterday, right after you left the bar, Lizárraga's friend showed up."

"Perú?"

"Yeah, Perú." Karina sipped her coffee. "We didn't talk much because the bar was packed, but the guy seems cool."

"Can I have a glass of water?" Comanche asked, his mouth dry and bitter.

She stood up and got a pitcher of cold water from the fridge.

The cold water did him good, refreshed him. He had to go. Calamaro was finishing with "La parte de adelante" on the stereo, giving way to a singer he'd never heard before. An Italian, Dalida; the song was "Ciao Amore, Ciao," a song Runcho liked, according to Karina, but one she thought was dramatic. Her playlist had a bit of everything; she'd delete what she didn't care for.

9.

Comanche arrived at the alleyway behind Ilusiones a couple of minutes early. Neither Papito nor Consorte were there. Just the kitchen staff of neighboring restaurants – cooks, waiters, and bus boys sitting around eating out of takeout containers. A couple of delivery bikes chained to racks and some boxes of cooking oil, beers, and sodas piled up against a grease trap, and an ad hoc army of broken chairs and tables waiting for the garbage truck.

Comanche leaned against a Honda Civic with a flat tire and faded black paint. He wiped the lenses of his aviator sunglasses with his shirt; they had fogged up from the humidity that typically predicted rain later in the day. He lit a cigarette. One drag. Another. And another. Consorte came out of Ilusiones, and a black Cadillac, with windows just as dark, turned the corner into the alleyway, slowed down, and moved forward until it stopped. A man got out of the passenger seat wearing Prada shades that covered half his face, wide burnt caramel-colored pants, rings, gold chains like an Olympic medalist, and comically oversized white basketball Nikes that looked like they belonged to an astronaut. A woman stepped out of the driver's side, wearing a green military camouflage t-shirt, combat boots, and a shaved head. Both greeted Consorte. The man turned to Comanche and stated, rather than asked: "Who are you?"

Comanche nonplussed said skip the formalities; they both knew who the other was and why they were there.

"Comanche, Papito, Papito, Comanche," intervened Consorte, motioning to one and then the other with both his hands and face.

"Alright, alright," Papito said, "that's better."

"Here, my friend Comanche," Consorte spoke up, "is looking for Gitano and Runcho. He's a loyal brother and knows the rules of the game."

"So, what are you, bro?" Papito asked. "Cop, private dick, what?"

"Listen, Mr. Papito," Comanche said, taking a step forward, "I collaborate with the police, period. That's all you need to know. Now, are we going to do what we came to do, or are we leaving it at that?"

"Take is easy, bro, easy, that shit don't work with me."

"You gonna help me? Yes, or no?"

"Sure thing, whatever."

"Alright. I'm listening," said Comanche, relaxing his stance a bit.

"So, that motherfucker Gitano..."

They had a rivalry over the coke market in Miami Beach that began years ago. Any turf that Papito conquered, Gitano tried to snatch away. Papito did the same with Gitano's turf. Sometimes

Gitano's people clashed with Papito's, but the two never faced off directly; their men did the dirty work. In one of those fights, down in the South Pointe area, which usually ended with a few stitches at the urgent care or black eyes and broken noses. One time a bullet slipped out from one of Gitano's men. Who fired it? No one ever knew, but it was very likely Runcho. He had just started with Gitano, and from the moment he arrived, he wanted to make his mark. For example, Gitano's men switched from knives to guns. The stray bullet hit Papito's brother, Nené, splattering his brains over the asphalt, leaving a stain that looked like a map of the Dominican Republic. He died instantly.

"Anyone?" asked Comanche, offering up his pack of Marlboros. The girl with the shaved head and combat boots took one. Papito waved his hand 'no.'

No cops came. South Pointe was at that point away from South Beach proper, it didn't have the beautiful park or the overpriced restaurants it had now. Everyone bolted as fast as they could. For the obvious reasons, Papito didn't report it and mourned his brother in an impromptu wake with his men at the warehouse where they kept their merch. They cremated him. From that day on Papito had a price on Gitano's head but there were no more fights between their crews – Gitano scaling back and keeping his business on Flamingo Park and Casa de Muñecas.

"Casa de Muñecas? The titty bar on Washington?" asked Comanche.

"Yeah," Papito said. "Only there. They're not at Flamingo anymore."

"Hold on," said Comanche, "how do you know they're not at Flamingo?"

"I'm on their shit. How they move. Where they move. Down to the millimeter."

"What do you know of Runcho?"

"Same as you. He's MIA," said Papito, adding that he knew Da Vinci was dead too.

"And why is Runcho MIA?"

"That's something *you* need to investigate, bro. He hasn't been seen anywhere."

"Okay. Give me details about Casa de Muñecas."

"That's also something you need to investigate. Go to the bar, order a private dance. Ask the girl for some coke."

Comanche rubbed his face, trying to organize and process the information to see if he could extract more details.

"You know what, bro? Papito asked.

"Tell me."

"I'll take that cigarette after all."

Comanche extended the pack to Papito; the woman passing it up this time but telling Papito they were pressed for time and had to leave.

"Alright," Papito said to Comanche. "I've talked too much."

"A couple more things."

"What things?"

"Where can I find Gitano? What's his name?"

"Don't know his name. And the only place that comes to mind is Muñecas."

"And Runcho?"

"Don't know shit about that motherfucker."

"Okay then."

"I do have one thing," Papito warned, already seated in the passenger seat.

"What thing?"

"Watch out for the Croat."

"What?"

"At Muñecas, bro, watch out for the Croat at the bar. Be careful." The Cadillac's engine started and drove off. Comanche and Consorte entered Ilusiones; the latter handing Comanche the Glock from the cupboard and the copy of *Revólver* with the Scarface article by Wild Cat.

"Why do they call this guy Papito?"

"He came like that from the factory, brother," said Consorte.

Papito and Nené grew up with their grandmother in a shack in the Cristo Rey neighborhood of the Dominican Republic, the three of them crammed together on a mattress laid on the floor, under a corrugated iron roof with a bare light bulb hanging from a wire and windows covered with black garbage bags. She used to call them that: my Papito and my Nené. There was no father. No mother. They were children of different men, whom they, of course, never met. While the mother was alive, the four of them occupied the mattress in the shack. But one night, the woman didn't come. The next night neither. And so on. On the corners of Cristo Rey, shrouded in shapeless columns of smoke, Papito and Nené learned, at that tender age when they should be throwing a baseball around, to defend themselves and watch their backs with razor blades or broken bottles. Although Papito stood out as the fiercer of the two: there wasn't a day they didn't come back to the shack without leaving a couple of black eyes on the corner.

"He arrived here with that noble title from the DR."

"Ah, he's tough."

"Tough as hell, brother," said Consorte. He'd only seen him bash a guy's face in one time. A business deal fell through that Consorte was involved in, and Papito asked him to reserve Ilusiones for a private meeting with those involved. There were six or seven plus the woman with the shaved head. He knew who had fucked up. He confronted him. The shaved-headed woman ordered everyone to grab a chair and form a circle. In the center, on a chair with his hands tied behind him, sat the guy. Papito was given a chair and stood beside him. Papito became a wild animal, an enraged bull, and the guy was dragged away, unconscious. He lost an eye and now walks around Miami Beach with a pirate patch, talking to himself because the beating left him insane. "That's why you can't play dirty with him."

"Calm down. You know me. That's not my style."

"Baldy's tough too," said Consorte. "She's Papito's main bodyguard. Former UFC fighter or some such shit."

"I better go," said Comanche, "thank you. I owe you one."

"That's what we're here for, brother."

10.

"Comanche."

"Officer," responded Comanche on the phone.

"I was about to call you, I got news."

"Me too, you first."

"Aramís Bocanegra, that's Gitano's name," said Pérez, pleased with himself. "I have his address too."

"Good, I got something big too, we gotta meet."

"When? Today?"

"No, tomorrow, early though," said Comanche without further details. He wanted to visit Casa de Muñecas first to see the layout and figure out his next moves.

"Let's do Los Latinos for breakfast."

"Perfect," said Comanche, "and another thing."

"Yeah?"

"What was the name of the song that was playing in Da Vinci's apartment?"

"The Italian one?"

"Yeah, that one."

"Let me see, I jotted it down in the report…"

"Okay."

"Ciao, Amore, Ciao."

"Sung by?"

"Dalida, why?"

"Just out of curiosity," though Comanche's mind strayed, imagining Runcho jamming to that song in front of Karina, getting horny thinking about fucking Da Vinci up the ass later.

At the front desk, Skinny asked him if he knew how much longer he'd be staying, so he could let La Cara de Trapo know when to clean the room. Peak tourist season was upon them and the rooms would book quickly. Comanche simply didn't know. He was still in the thick of it, but once he had an idea, he'd let him know. In his room, he placed the Glock on the nightstand and called Romero to give him an update – letting his handler know he'd given Pérez a piece of his mind for the lie – something Romero did not like. Then he texted Mariolys, undressed, lit a cigarette and sat on the toilet to read Wild Cat's article.

By Wild Cat

Long Live Scarface

One of the classics of local cinema is Scarface. The film, starring Al Pacino, defined a new era and a new profile of immigrant.

One of the best-selling souvenirs in the shops on Washington Avenue, Ocean Drive, and Collins is the t-shirt with Tony Montana's face and the caption "The World is Yours." Montana, the role played by Al Pacino in the film **Scarface** by Brian De Palma, is a popular youth icon in Miami.

Scarface is one of De Palma's greatest hits, and it starts with the historic Mariel boatlift, during which, from April to October 1980, Fidel Castro sent about 125,000 Cubans to seek refuge in Florida, emptying the island's jails and mental health facilities. Brian De Palma portrayed Tony Montana as one of these refugees—a vulgar, ordinary, and ambitious character who quickly became Miami's number one drug dealer. With or without some scenes, the film seems monotonous and lacks a greater plot other than snorting cocaine, laundering money, and shooting guns. If we watch the three-hour **Scarface** today, we might say that the effort isn't worth it. It's a film that hasn't aged well, and even setting aside Al Pacino's masterful performance, it's jarring to see a Marielito played by an actor who doesn't speak Spanish (if it were contemporary, Montana would likely be Ricardo Darín). But we shouldn't throw it all away; remember that Miami, back then, was no less sordid or petty than depicted in the film: its murder rate was the highest in the country (six to seven per day), at least one of the bills in every Miamian's wallet had been used to snort cocaine, and the cultural clash between Anglos and Latinos was unsustainable. Alex Daoud, Miami Beach mayor in 1985, recounts in his memoir **Sins of South Beach**, how he would go out at night with police to hunt Latinos to beat them up and put them in black garbage bags.

De Palma's **Scarface** is a remake of Howard Hughes' **Scarface**, a 1932 black-and-white film that has little to do with Marielitos and Miami, as it more closely deals with the early years of Al Capone on the streets of Chicago. Hughes' Scarface is an adaptation of a novel with the same title, written by "a certain" Armitage Trail in 1929.

In the 1920s, when the hardboiled genre was at its peak, pulp magazines featured stories by a sixteen-year-old who used the pen name Armitage Trail. Behind Trail was Maurice Coons (1902 – 1930), a young man who, at fifteen, left school to dedicate himself to writing because nothing else interested him. Coons spent part of his youth on the streets of Chicago, moving in the underworld, dazzled by the Sicilian mafia. At that time, The Chicago Outfit was at its peak, and Al Capone's figure was emerging within the organization. According to urban legend, it was during those years that, after leaving a bar, Capone received two knife wounds that left the scar that led to his nickname: Scarface.

Both myth and legend, Al Capone inspired Maurice Coons to write the novel **Scarface** about the story of Tony Guarino, a gangster who started in Chicago and became the greatest mobster in the United States. The 156-page novel, which pays a small but significant homage to Capone—though with an unhappy ending—was acclaimed by both the public and critics, and the author quickly sold the rights to adapt it to the screen. Fame and recognition leave a good taste; Coons knew this firsthand, as he was soon seen in a luxury car with a chauffeur, drinking excessively often, and dining at fine tables. However, this bon vivant lifestyle took its toll very early: a fatal heart attack took Coons at 28, weighing over 300 pounds, and he never saw the adaptation of his novel (Al Capone did).

In addition to **Scarface**, Armitage Trail also wrote **The Thirteenth Guest**, and despite his brief life, his literary contribution has transcended time and is now recognized as one of the essential and pioneering voices of American hardboiled literature.

REVÓLVER
EDICIONES

Revólver Ediciones is a publication by undocumented writers and journalists clandestinely operating within Miami Beach.

11.

The entrance to Casa de Muñecas was guarded by a grim-faced bouncer in a dark suit and tie. Behind him was a tunnel with neon stars on the walls and a ceiling that led to a room with chairs covered in a kind of burgundy synthetic leather. The air was filled with sweet perfume, sweaty bodies, and cigarette smoke, and there was an all-you-can-eat buffet of plump asses split in half by red, black, violet, and white G-strings. In the center, a small stage where the DJ introduced La Gata Fiera, a woman who removed a cat costume and was left only with a sequin mask, while Juan Luis Guerra's smooth voice sang "Bachata Rosa."

"What would you like to drink?" the bartender asked.

"Bacardí with Coke and lime," said Comanche, taking a stool on the corner of the bar that let him see whole floor.

On the opposite corner, a man with a sentry's gaze, straw-colored hair, and a fitted black shirt in the Armani style that accentuated his shell-like pectorals, was gesticulating and giving orders to the staff. His eyes darted from one woman with a thong-split ass to another. "Watch out for the Croat at the bar," Comanche remembered Papito's words. This must be him; his intuition was right. Who he didn't see was Gitano.

"Here you go, sir," said the bartender, leaving the rum cocktail on the bar in front of him. Comanche, draining half in one swig, asked for another with less ice.

The goon on the other side, the Croat maybe, kept his vigil, choreographing even more movement with his hands and eyes between the dancers and clients, who sat at tables drinking and smoking, the grey fog from lit cigarettes and ashtrays clouding the air in the room.

"Who is this good-smelling man?" Comanche heard a woman ask. He'd given his neck a generous spritz of Brut before he left his room at El Bikini. She wore a matching leopard-print bra and G-string. He motioned the bartender for his third cocktail and taking her by the waist, asked her what she was drinking. Casually, she took his hand off and leaned into the bar to order her usual, a Cosmo.

"No touching baby, no touching," she told him. "If you want, after we drink these, I'll give you a lap dance you'll never forget."

Comanche didn't care for titty bars, avoided them, when possible, it was impossible to surround himself with fine women like that, breathing heavy in his ear, shaking hips and rubbing their large asses on him, and not be able to touch them.

"I'm Ruby," she said. "What's your name, handsome?"

"Roberto," Comanche improvised.

"Ooh, Rob," Ruby said, "very masculine."

"And yours, very erotic," he said into her ear, following along.

They toasted and Comanche had to remind himself to pace the drinks, he was working after all. Any drinks that would follow would be even more loaded on rum and less cola – he'd shipwreck himself with the booze if he didn't tighten up. He'd let the ice melt, spilling a bit here and there when no one would notice.

"You're on vacation?"

"Business trip."

"Ooh, you're a businessman?"

"That's right."

"Businessmen turn me on."

"Your ass turns me on."

"Oh my, how rude… I fucking love a man like that."

"Thanks."

"Wanna go in a private room so we can have more fun?"

"How much more fun could we possibly have?"

"I'll dance for you, let's get another round."

"Hmm… my night is kinda short without blow and I'm out."

"Don't you worry about that, let's go to a private room."

Ruby called over a waiter. They'd be going to a private room and would need the deluxe package, same drinks as before.

The private room was soundproof, had the ripe cantaloupe smell of sweaty ass, crimson red carpeting, a few chairs separated by a long, dark brown rectangular wooden table with thick legs. A 75" wall-mounted flatscreen flashed videos of topless women on white sand beaches. Ruby instructed him to get comfortable while they waited for their cocktails and told him the rules: each song she danced was 30 bucks – minimum three songs – and no touching. If he touched her, she'd hit an alarm that would summon security.

There was a knock at the door, it was the guy from the corner of the bar, the Croat maybe, his straw-colored hair brighter up close, eyes still like a sentry's. He didn't talk, only stared at Comanche, and slipped something into Ruby's hands. The waiter was with him, their drinks in hand and a crystal bowl full of olives, compliments of the bar.

"You've hardly touched your drink," Ruby said, looking at his glass. Even with spilling as much as he could, whenever he could, he still had half of the drink left.

"I told you baby," he replied. "Without a bit of coke, I'm worthless, my night ends early."

"Oh my god, you're all the same."

"All of us?"

"Yeah, all you businessmen. Worthless without blow."

"Well, you'd know more about that than me."

"Fine, I guess every problem has a solution," she said as she extended her hand over the table, dropping a small red baggie on it. "That's yours, put it away, I didn't see shit."

Comanche feigned surprise, putting it away in his shirt pocket and excused himself, time to refuel. He closed himself in a stall, spilling what was left of his drink down the toilet. He opened the red baggie, it was the same type of Ziploc that was sold across Flamingo Park; he was tempted to take a bump, let it shoot up his nose and explode in his brain, filling him with a burst of adrenaline. But he only dabbed the tip of his pinky in it, rubbing it across his tongue, numbing it. Then he peed. When he came out, he saw the straw-colored hair guy from earlier washing his hands, their eyes crossed. Comanche raised a brow at him. It was the Croat, no doubt about that and he was probably following him. Watch out for the Croat he'd been told. Without thinking, he palmed the Glock tucked behind him, he felt better, and continued to the private room. Ruby, on all fours, greeted him in there, her ass held high, a monument of flesh. She was an altar; she was a fucking throne.

"Ready to have fun?" she asked without moving.

"It's better if I go," he said, pulling three $20's from his wallet, "for the drinks, I have an important meeting with a client at 8 a.m."

Ruby got up, pissed she'd wasted her evening. If the guy outside, the Croat, saw that he left so soon, he'd be pissed too. They didn't like to waste their time either. Comanche paid her no mind, and taking advantage that the door was still open, he slipped out. On the stage, La Leona del Trópico danced to Maná's "El Muelle de San Blas," her bra between her teeth, her breasts, like oversized fists, bouncing in rhythm, her cinnamon-colored nipples tracing through the smoke-filled air. He picked up his pace amongst the G-stringed asses and businessmen who'd eventually get to enjoy one of Ruby's memorable dances. He gauged his distance to the exit, should be easy, the Croat was nowhere in sight, but he also didn't turn back to look at the bar, didn't want the bartender to see him either. Outside, the grim-faced bouncer and some dude were chatting and smoking cigars. Comanche knocked into them accidentally, the force causing him to lose his balance and almost eat the pavement. The dude caught him, helped straighten him up and without letting go asked him, "You okay man, you okay?"

His skin was olive, his hair was neatly pulled back in a pony-tail, his eyes large, as were the gold hoops hanging from his ears. It was Gitano and his heart began beating at full speed – he couldn't fuck this up, he had to fight any impulse, any urge. He thanked him, finished straightening himself up and walked out of Casa de Muñecas, the doors closing behind him, muting the music... *Sola en el olvido, sola con su espíritu, sola con el sol y el mar.*

12.

His morning shower was a parade of mental Polaroids... the fat asses from Casa de Muñecas; Ruby's held high and spread on that table in the private room; Karina's thong on the floor of her efficiency, her firm ass held tight inside her work pants... jerking himself while pulling on his balls covered with mentholated suds, stopping only after shooting his load down the drain. He got dressed quickly and headed out to Los Latinos.

"Try the *baleadas*," said Officer Pérez.

"I've never had them."

"Try them, you won't regret it."

Even though Pérez insisted, Comanche preferred eggs and

a Nicaraguan tamale, letting the waitress with the "Here, we're all proud Cholos!" t-shirt know. What they both agreed on was the coffee: hot, black, no milk, no sugar, no type of sweetener.

"Aramís Bocanegra," Pérez said, "lives on Lennox Avenue, close to Lincoln Road..."

"I saw him yesterday," Comanche interrupted.

"How's that, what the fuck do you mean?"

One of his snitches said that Gitano not only controlled Flamingo Park, but the strip club Casa de Muñecas too, that he'd been seen hanging around there frequently. He'd stopped by the night before and his guy wasn't wrong. He even had a little baggie of coke, red like the Flamingo ones, "red bullets" like they called them. Gitano's guy inside was a dude known as the Croat. He didn't have a photo of him, wasn't possible to take one since he had to bolt quickly out of there – but he was easy to describe and identify if Pérez wanted him to sit down with a sketch artist.

"Fuck, Comanche," a visibly pleased Pérez said. "This is good."

Gitano's business was cornered into the titty bar, they'd have to focus on that as their new target.

"How did that meet-up go, exactly?"

"I was on my way out, I literally tripped over him at the door," Comanche said. "He was nice, kept me from falling flat on my face. I thanked him. And I meant it too."

"Alright, but wait," said Pérez. "We need to think about our next steps."

"*Baleadas* and *nacatamal*, gentlemen," said the waitress holding their breakfasts.

"Eggs over here, please," motioned Comanche.

She put the plates in front of them and refilled their coffees. If they needed anything else, she was at their service.

"Okay, let's think."

They agreed on Comanche tailing Gitano, from his front door and through all his comings and goings – gathering as much evidence as possible so they could bring him in and arrest him. They couldn't risk Gitano bonding out in a couple of hours and returning to the comforts of his apartment on Lennox. In tandem, Pérez and his task force would infiltrate Muñecas to see what they could turn up and investigate the Croat.

"Pass me the pepper?" asked Comanche.

"Here you go," said the officer, handing him the shaker. "And Runcho? Don't tell me you saw Runcho last night as well."

"No, that fucker's disappearance is still a mystery. Like the earth swallowed him whole, not even his ex has heard from him. Nor my informant who told me about Gitano. No one."

"Well, next time order the *baleadas*, you won't regret it."

"You getting a kickback for each one they sell?"

Winking, "you won't regret it."

"Alright, next time."

13.

Gitano's building was Art Deco in style, white, with pink flamingos and melon-colored bas relief starfish on the entrance arch. His apartment was on the second floor, with a terrace overlooking Lincoln Road. Comanche had been standing in front of that 1950s Miami Beach postcard since leaving Los Latinos. Fortunately, the corner was shaded by trees, which, along with the Marlboros, made the wait more bearable. Gitano left his house after Comanche had lost count of how many cigarettes he had smoked. He was dressed in Nike, sporty, carrying a small brown leather bag on his shoulder. He headed in the opposite direction of Lincoln Road, and Comanche hurried after him, keeping a safe distance. The entire walk was in a straight line to Española Way, where the olive-skinned thug entered a unit through the back door, the one used by employees and suppliers. Comanche circled around to identify the place – it was Café Piccolo. He went inside.

"Can I get a table?"

"Anywhere," replied the waiter, folding napkins, without looking up – already walking over to take his order. Comanche didn't take off his Ray-Bans as he looked the place over: four occupied tables, a hallway leading to the bathroom, behind the Formica counter, a skinny man with a hooked nose and a chin like the bow of a ship was talking on the phone, mixing Italian, Spanish, and English. On the tables, small plastic figurines of the Tower of Pisa, and on one wall, a charcoal sketch of the canals of Venice. No trace of Gitano.

"How can I help you?" asked the waiter.

"Coffee and two croquetas, please."

"We don't have croquettes," he replied. "Croissants are our specialty."

"Well then, coffee, black, and a croissant."

Nothing. No hint of El Gitano anywhere and Comanche had been perched in his spot for 10 minutes already. There was the possibility that he'd come in that way because he was actually an employee there, worked in the kitchen or something, hence why he didn't see him in the front of the house – but there was a slim chance of that being true he thought. Not with the cash he was bringing in with his red bullets. The guy with a chin like the bow of a ship hung up and walked towards the hallway leading to the bathroom.

"Sugar or any sweetener?" asked the waiter, holding up a tray with his croissant and steaming cup of coffee.

"No, nothing."

"Anything else, sir?"

"Where's your bathroom?"

"That way," he said, pointing down the hallway.

The coffee was awful. Shit water. But he was right about the croissant when he said it was the house specialty. The skinny guy with the hooked nose didn't come out of the hallway, so Comanche decided to explore that area and got up from the table. At the end, against the wall, there were boxes of Coca-Cola, Fanta, Sprite, and Perriers, along with Tuscan wines and olive oils; and across from the bathroom door, there was another door with a small sign that said, 'Staff Only.' Gitano and the skinny guy had to be in there. Comanche stayed there, trying to hear something, but all he could catch was a faint, muffled murmur from the other side.

Back at his table, he ordered a bottle of water and another croissant. The skinny guy returned to his spot behind the counter, but there was still no sign of Gitano. However, someone familiar came out of the Staff Only door. He watched closely as the person came out of the bathroom and went back into the Staff Only area. Observing him in profile, he had no doubts: judging by the build and haircut, it was the Croat. Ever since he arrived at the Piccolo, Comanche had a sense that the little café wasn't completely unfamiliar, and he remembered Karina mentioning that Runcho used to come there in the mornings for breakfast. Without asking for his tab, Comanche left a $20 on the table beneath his croissant plate and left.

"Hi," answered Karina on the third ring.

"You sure Runcho ate breakfast at the Café Piccolo every day?"

"Yeah, the Italian spot on Española. Why?"

"Alright, I'll tell you later."

Comanche circled the café, peeked through the back door where Gitano had entered, and likely the Croat too, because during the whole time he was sitting there devouring croissants, he hadn't seen him enter through the front door. The area was clear: just brooms, buckets, and rags. He pulled out the Glock he had tucked between his back and his Levi's, gripped it, made sure he wasn't in the angle of the security camera, knocked on the door, and ran to hide between the green garbage bins that allowed him visibility of the Piccolo without being seen. The Croat opened the door, looked around, but didn't see anyone. Comanche took out his phone and snapped a photo. The Croat lit a joint, took a couple of puffs, and a warm breeze carrying the smell of marijuana brushed against Comanche's nostrils. Gitano came out to ask who had knocked, and Comanche took a photo of the two of them.

"Someone dropping off flyers," said the Croat, kicking at the papers with the week's promotions that had piled up on the floor.

"Come in, asshole," said Gitano, a bit annoyed. "You can finish your J later; we have a lot left to do."

When they'd gone inside, and the door closed firmly behind them, Comanche put the Glock back in his waistband and walked quickly away from the back alley. On the corner of Meridian and Española Way he texted Officer Pérez the photos and immediately, his phone rang.

"We got them," Comanche greeted him. "We got the sons of bitches."

"What do you mean, Comanche," replied Pérez. "What do you mean?"

Comanche filled him in.

Pérez would get his team to look up the Croat in their databases and see what they could find. He'd meet Comanche at Los Latinos in an hour to plan their next moves.

He didn't have enough time to get back to El Bikini, so he walked over to Flamingo Park instead, sat on a bench across from a tennis court where an instructor was working with a pair of young kids decked out in Lacoste gear and Rafael Nadal sneakers. He lit up a Marlboro and called Romero to bring him up to speed on the case.

"And Runcho?"

"Nothing on that, Boss."

Then he called Mariolys, who sounded happy at the sound of his voice. They agreed on La Carreta, again, for a *carne con papa* lunch, whenever he got back.

14.

"Two cortaditos," Pérez asked at the coffee window outside Los Latinos. The restaurant was packed, and they wouldn't be able to talk inside. Not in that din anyways. Outside was better. A warm breeze flowed over the spacious sidewalk.

"Want one?" Comanche asked Pérez, holding his Marlboros out, but the officer declined.

The Croat was Julien Kovasich Echevarría, sentenced to five years in prison for credit card and identity theft at gas stations in Kendall and Homestead. His sentence was reduced to three years for good behavior, and he was also serving a year of probation and community service, which was currently in effect. Nothing was apparently found regarding Café

Piccolo and its owner, Luciano Piccini, the skinny guy with the hooked nose. It was important to emphasize 'apparently' because Piccini owned several properties in Miami Beach, one of which housed Casa de Muñecas, although he was not listed in the business incorporation papers. Pérez had two men watching the front and back doors of the Piccolo. Something was brewing there alright; the next day, early in the morning, they would intervene. The order from his superior was already authorized, and that night one of his men would infiltrate Muñecas. Simultaneously, with the raid at the Piccolo, they would grab Gitano at his house and bring him to the Miami Beach Police Department for questioning. They did not yet have complete evidence implicating him directly for an arrest, but he was a clear suspect for drug trafficking.

"What if you get nothing out of him and have to let him go?" Comanche asked. "Don't you think he'd get wise to what we're up to and then the case would be fucked?"

"Yeah, you're right," said Pérez, but they already had something on Casa de Muñecas. They'd sold Comanche coke there, the Croat had, that was irrefutable. If Gitano walked, they'd take down the operation at the strip club and arrest the Croat. That was something. They were in a good spot. They would find something on Gitano soon, and they had him under surveillance, he wouldn't be able to keep his shit up or skip town.

"Okay, what time is the raid on the café?"

"As early as possible." Pérez would need Comanche situated inside scoping the restaurant, ahead of the task force, to green-light the raid at the best moment.

"They open at eight."

"Then we'll be in place by then."

Although it was still early and the night in South Beach could offer him a lot, Comanche preferred to go to his room, with a stop at the Art Deco Market to buy Coca-Cola and limes to make himself some fiestas. At El Bikini, Skinny was watching a Miami Heat game on a small TV he had installed above the counter. The team was fighting for a spot in the playoffs, Skinny said, wearing a Dwyane Wade jersey, and asked Comanche if he wanted to watch the game with him; it had just started, and they could order Papa John's pizzas. Comanche thanked him but wasn't interested in basketball. Instead, he asked Skinny for some ice for his drinks.

The red bullet on the table, next to the Bacardí bottle, was a temptation too great for Comanche, but he decided to avoid it. He took off his shoes, shirt, and Levi's, filled his glass halfway with rum, added a splash of Coca-Cola, half a lime, and ice, then collapsed onto the bed in his underwear and lit a Marlboro. The room lacked a sound system to play Héctor Lavoe's songs and provide some company, but in its absence, he turned on the TV and left it on the channel where the Miami Heat were playing. He wasn't interested in the game, didn't know who they were playing against, but the commentator and the roar of the crowd made enough noise.

His phone vibrated, Officer Pérez's name flashing on the screen.

"Hello, Officer."

His undercovers staking out the Piccolo, had seen Gitano and the Croat leave and go to Casa de Muñecas. There they split. Gitano to his apartment. They saw him sit on the balcony with a MacBook Pro, drink a Modelo and smoke a Cuban he bit the end of, spitting the brown nub over the railing before lighting it. He didn't go out again and his guys stayed there all night.

"That was all," Pérez said. "Anything I hear, I'll call you, if not, we proceed as planned tomorrow at 8 a.m."

The phone vibrated again, not a second passing since hanging up on the cop. It was Karina.

"*Che*, you still around?"

"Yeah, still."

The *Revólver* guys were dropping the latest issue at the Al Capone the next day at their Literatura Callejera event. The new edition was dedicated to Lizárraga and Wild Cat had asked her to invite him.

"At what time?"

"I dunno, around 8 or 9."

"Okay."

Comanche put the phone down on the nightstand, downed what was left of his fiesta, and turned off the television and the lights.

15.

At Café Piccolo only one table was taken. It was a couple and Luciano Piccini, sitting behind the counter, was focused on his accounting ledger, a calculator beside him and a mixed pile of receipts and invoices from his vendors.

"A croissant and an American coffee," Comanche asked a waiter. Then he texted Pérez to let him know he was inside.

"Same here, working out the final details," responded Pérez from his squad car parked outside Gitano's place.

"Green light whenever you want," Comanche texted back.

Four undercovers walked in, badges held high, led by Officer Delphine Laurent. They asked the couple and Comanche to leave and for Piccini and the waiter to drop whatever they were doing and to sit, hands on top of the table, palms up. Comanche walked out, then ran to the back. Four squad cars had the alleyway pinned, a dozen uniforms, guns drawn toward the door while two others knocked on it with battering rams.

"Get back," a uniform told Comanche.

The door came down.

The uniforms went in.

The Croat was waiting for them on the other side, a snug-nosed Smith & Wesson .44 pointed at them. For a moment frozen in time, everything was bullets, sounds of bullets: bang, bang, bang. The first bullet hit Officer Gamboa in the forearm; the second hit the Croat in the knee. Crawling, he tried to reach some sacks of rice and flour to seek cover behind them, but on the way, he received two shots in the stomach and one in the jugular and fell convulsing, face up, like a frog on a laboratory table with his abdomen open: intestines, guts, entrails. A viscous, chocolate-colored stream oozed from the hole that had perforated his neck from side to side. Someone else was with the Croat; Comanche couldn't see who, only hearing the officers shout not to shoot, the target wasn't resisting and wasn't armed. The situation calmed down, the police took full control, and they pulled out a subject handcuffed, hiding under the brim of a Yankees cap. He was going to cooperate; he was going to help. When they took off the cap to put him in the car, Comanche was finally able to see who it was. Runcho.

In front of the Piccolo, inside a patrol car, Piccini and the waiter were doing their darnest to make themselves as small as possible to hide from passersby and neighbors gathering on the sidewalks to see what was happening. Gamboa was taken away in an ambulance, on a stretcher, with an oxygen mask on his face. The Croat was taken away in another Miami Beach Fire & Rescue ambulance, wrapped in a black body bag, zippered up from head to toe. The Piccolo was surrounded by yellow tape: "Crime Scene, Police Don't Cross."

Gitano asked politely if he could grab a pair of comfortable shoes from his closet, grabbing a pair of thick-soled, yellow New Balances. He didn't say another word. One of the cops handcuffed him. Two other cops hooked their arms under his and took him to the squad car outside. Gitano kept his eyes so low it was as if he was sweeping the sidewalk with his vision.

16.

The interviews were done at the same time. Runcho in one room with Officer Díaz. Gitano in another with Officer Delphine Laurent. Runcho had been living at the Piccolo since beating up Karina, rooming with the Croat who couldn't find anyone to rent him anything due to his record. They'd brought in a pair of mattresses and a TV.

He didn't know about Lizárraga's death until the wake; someone mentioned it to him. The night he hit Comanche at Lizárraga's house was because he went in to look for any evidence of his girlfriend's infidelity. It wasn't the first time he had done this; once he found a sweater belonging to that "slut" and didn't say anything because he didn't want to come off as an insecure loser. Instead, he hit her. She was in the shower, he tried to seduce her, 'not today, Runcho, not today, I'm not in the mood.' He knew she wasn't in the mood because she had been having sex all afternoon with Lizárraga, and that's why he gave her the black eye. When Da Vinci died, things became complicated for him to return, and he emphasized making it clear that he didn't kill him. The guy died alone; Runcho thought it was an orgasm, but it went on and on, never coming back from the climax. He then asked to take a break, not wanting what he was about to say to be recorded.

Officer Díaz told him to go to hell and forced him to continue, so he said it didn't matter, he would make it clear anyway, he wasn't gay, he didn't like men, it disgusted him. Even thinking about something in his ass was revolting, but when he drank too much vodka with Da Vinci, and they snorted some red bullets, they fucked wildly. He penetrated him. And Da Vinci, in doggy style, screaming:

'fuck me, fucker, *my* fucker.' When he learned that the police were at the scene lifting fingerprints and seized the sports bag with drugs, he thought that when things calmed down, he'd flee to Georgia, with Fiorito, the one with the big gun who had also been with him in the Flamingo Park business but who always knew he'd make some money and leave Miami to start another life, which he had done a few days earlier. And yes, yes, he admitted it: he was Gitano's right-hand man, but only in Flamingo Park; in Casa de Muñecas, it was the Croat.

Gitano, with his bloodshot eyes and olive skin, told Officer Laurent that he had nothing to say to a woman, especially if she was Black. And even more so, if she was Haitian. Damn Haitian. She should go back to whatever shithole town she was from and do her voodoo. She tasered him in the ribs, he spat at her, and Delphine Laurent elbowed him in the face. The officers observing from the other side of the one-way glass ran in to intervene.

In the end, he admitted to being responsible for the illegal activities he was accused of, including being the owner of the cocaine packed in Ziploc bags found by the task force officers in the back room of the Piccolo. There were three Smith & Wessons like the one the Croat used, and four Glocks accompanying them, in a locked trunk they had to pry open. And several thick bundles of hundred-dollar bills at his house. He did not deny his responsibility; he detested this shitty country, this shitty society, these shitty politicians, and if he could do anything else to screw over this shitty city, he would.

"What about Luciano Piccini and the fucking waiter?" asked Comanche.

"Piccini rented them the space," explained Pérez, and that he was making more on that rent alone than he ever was with the croissants. He was involved in Casa de Muñecas too – now closed and under investigation. The waiter was complicit, knowing everything that went down in that place, his silence bought by the C-notes the Croat would stuff into his jacket.

"How's the cop who got shot?"

"Gamboa? Good, he's in stable condition. Nothing vital was hit. They should release him tomorrow. Couple of days of rest and he'll be right back at it."

Comanche scanned the walls of Pérez's office: medals, certificates, recognitions, diplomas, honor plaques, an American flag, and portraits of El Gitano, Runcho, the Croat, and Piccini. On the desk, in a silver frame with white gold accents, was a photo from years ago – back when Romero was a solid son of a bitch, built like a brick house and sported Pharaoh sideburns and a lush mane – of Pérez and Romero at Pérez's graduation ceremony from the Miami Beach Police Academy. Pérez, with his endless smile, was holding his diploma, the honors distinction in gold foil. Romero, with a puffed chest and pure pride, perhaps seeing in Pérez the son he and Nancy were never fortunate enough to bring into the world due to the endless patrol shifts or because of his womanizing ways. That's what the police academy gossips whispered in the halls about his whoring around – lunches, coffees, pastries, and long hours behind closed doors with Samantha, his secretary, who wore knee-high black boots and had a long, curly, jet-black mane that swayed between her lower back and ass.

Comanche got up from the chair. Pérez offered to have a squad car take him to El Bikini, but he preferred to walk. However, he reminded Pérez not to forget what he promised when they agreed to work together: one of his men would take him to Little Havana, and Pérez said to count on it; by 9 in the morning, he would have someone stationed at El Bikini, waiting to do so.

The sun was baking the sidewalks outside the Miami Beach Police Department, the heat shimmer refracting the carnival of colorful towels on shoulders, six-packs of beer, and coolers heading toward the sea on the street. Comanche put on his Ray-Ban aviators, lit a Marlboro, and headed toward Ilusiones to return the Glock to Consorte and see if he could catch a couple of games with Chamizo. He would let him know he was coming; taking a few bucks from the kid wouldn't hurt either.

17.

"Cheers, Inspector," said Cabalito, clinking his Heineken bottle with Comanche's highball of rum, taking the opportunity to introduce him to Perú.

"Cheers," said Comanche.

"This is the new cashier at La Chismosa," Cabalito said, tapping Perú on the shoulder. "He just lost his job, and I needed to replace Lizárraga."

"Good for you, Perú," Comanche said. "And nice to meet you."

Perú told him that the pleasure was his, thanking Comanche for his work on the Lizárraga case. They had been good friends when Lizárraga got to Miami – matter of fact, Perú had become his first friend here. He was about to continue with his story but the lights at the bar went out and complete silence fell upon the crowd. Then, the gentle strumming of an acoustic guitar broke the silence… they would continue their convo later.

Eran tus ojos los que me atraían
me parecías un chico bestial
cuando te vi, no lo creía
me parecías un chico bestial

La Chica más pop de South Beach opened up Literatura Callejera, debuting her new hit, "El Chico Bestial," in an unplugged version. The whole band would play later.

Unlike other occasions when the neon lights brought life to the stage, this time it was limited to a spotlight that sprinkled tiny drops that looked like honey onto La Chica más pop, holding her guitar in a blue velvet armchair, wearing a denim jacket, red Chuck Taylors, and a T-shirt with the cover art of *Bares y fondas* by Los Fabulosos Cadillacs. Behind her, the outline of Al Capone's face on the wall. After the applause, Wild Cat took the stage and thanked the audience. It was a special night, very special, he corrected, dedicated to a colleague who was no longer physically present but would remain forever in their memory because he had left behind a great novel, *Ciudad Maldita*, which would soon be published under the *Revólver Ediciones* label. Gregorio Lizárraga, for those who did not know him, and simply Lizárraga for those who did, with that book was becoming the first author to write a work in Spanish in the Tropical Noir genre, a traditional and prominent genre in Miami established by Anglo authors, enduring for over 70 years. Before continuing with poetry readings by Lasticön and the signing of copies of the new issue of the magazine, Wild Cat would read a passage from *Ciudad Maldita*.

Comanche paid no attention to La Chica más pop de

South Beach and her guitar, nor to Wild Cat's words or the excerpt from *Ciudad Maldita*. His mind was on Romero and his stinky office in the complex painted in the muted yellows of a *flan* pudding on Flagler.

What time does he leave there, huh? He thought to himself.

At 9 a.m., one of Pérez's guys would pick him up. He was expected at 10 in the morning, on time, Romero had said with displeasure on the phone, as a new case was being delayed because of his stay at the beach. Comanche was starting to get fed up with Romero: the demands, the complaints; old fool. These days he'd worked directly with Pérez, relegated to a secondary role, made him flirt with the idea of picking up the phone and telling him to go to Hell. Yeah, back to the whore who'd given birth to him. He'd stay on in Miami Beach for a while, working on his own. He didn't do it. He wouldn't do it, at least for now. What he did was look around for Karina, wanting another rum, but she was with other customers. So, he tilted the glass, finished what little was left, and got up to go to the bathroom: he would finally pinch that bump from the little red baggie, the little red bullet.

DELIRIO SOUTH BEACH

(a couple of months later)

1.

Comanche felt his way across the nightstand, looking for his Marlboros. Then he sat up on the edge of the bed and lit up. The room smelled of sweat and sex. Mariolys lay naked next to him. She caved into him the night before, starting in his kitchenette at the Sweet Dreams hostel where they cut up potatoes, tomatoes, yellow onions in thick discs, and large chunks of sirloin. Comanche handled the rest, manning the frying pan that filled the place with the smell of soy sauce, vinegar, salt, and pepper. They listened to a live concert by Héctor Lavoe recorded at the Palladium in New York City. They opened a bottle of Bacardí Gold. He made three, four, five fiestas, and his Levi's and shirt came off, followed by her fake True Religion jeans and blouse.

After savoring the memory, the taste of her pussy in his mouth, his eyes rolled back in the remembered ecstasy amidst the sizable plumes of Marlboro smoke he exhaled, as he was readying himself to disconnect from the memory and get a pot of coffee going, his phone rang.

"Romero."

"Yes, Comanche, yes," Romero knew it was the weekend and before Comanche could bitch for being indisposed or too fucking drunk to comply, he told him it was an emergency.

"Of?"

"Officer Pérez."

"Again?" Comanche interrupted.

"I'm afraid so."

Comanche would leave that afternoon for Miami Beach, he already had the room at El Bikini, Pérez would grab him the following morning and give him the details.

Romero could only tell him it was a missing persons case. A policeman's son. Officer Pérez's direct supervisor and they did not want any media attention. They'd have to move quickly, discreetly.

"That's all, Nancy's waiting for me to go to Denny's for breakfast."

"Okay."

"Call a cab, Comanche and keep me in the loop."

Comanche dropped his butt into a nearby glass. A slice of lime floated on a tiny sliver of flat Coke in it. Just as he'd made his mind up to get up and get the coffee going, Mariolys hugged him from behind, kissing his neck, sliding her soft hand down between his thighs.

2.

Crossing the MacArthur Causeway, the asphalt artery connecting Miami Beach with the rest of the city, was something Comanche was liking more and more. From the moment he saw the megalithic cruise ships docked at the Port of Miami on Dodge Island on one side, and the mansions of Star Island where Enrique Iglesias, Lionel Richie, and the Estefans lived. Each time he made this trek, he felt the yellowed suburban Hell of the city melt away in his wake.

"Who the fuck are you supposed to be?" asked Comanche noticing Skinny as he walked into El Bikini. The front desk clerk was busy rearranging room keys on the little wooden board behind him.

"Bro, the Heat won yesterday, this is Wade's jersey!"

"Fucking clown."

"C'mon bro, we're in the playoffs as favorites to go all the way."

"Same room as always?" asked Comanche.

"Yeah man, La Cara de Trapo just cleaned it."

Comanche hung his three shirts in the closet, took his shoes off, then his Levi's which he placed on the table next to his aviators, and laid back on the bed to enjoy a smoke.

"Just got here," he told Mariolys on the phone.

"And I just got back from checking out the 1/1 on Flagler," she replied.

They hadn't been together long, hardly actually, but they had decided to move in together since she was sleeping over almost every night at the Sweet Dreams with him than at her own place. Comanche had been very clear about one thing: he didn't want kids. He wasn't capable of bringing someone into the world and the responsibility that it entailed.

"And?"

"It's cute," Mariolys said.

The best part was that it was close to Romero's agency and the Mall of the Americas where Mariolys would start working the following day at El Dolarazo. She was excited to start this new chapter of her life with him and had told him, choked up through teary eyes, squeezing his hand, that afternoon they'd gone to the mall for her to apply at the store. He waited for her outside, drinking a Coca-Cola next to a Disney carrousel – Donald Duck, Dumbo and Mickey Mouse circling over and over to "London Bridge is Falling Down." One kid was on it, jumping Donald to Dumbo, from Dumbo to Mickey, and from Mickey to Donald. She got the job on the spot and Mariolys wanted to celebrate. They went to La Carreta, sitting in the dining area instead of at the bar like they usually did for this special occasion. She ordered a *palomilla* steak, with *moros* and *maduros* with a mojito. He got the *pan con bistec* and an ice-cold Heineken.

"You can tell me all about it when I get back."

"I took a bunch of photos. Luz went with me."

"Your cousin?"

"Yeah man, who else?"

"Cool, ok, we'll talk."

Comanche hung up and went out for his Bustelo tin and Bacardí bottle to keep him company. One of the comforts he enjoyed while working in Miami Beach, was including the rum in the expense reports Romero reimbursed him.

3.

"Surprise, surprise, *Che*! What are you doing around here?"

"On a case," replied Comanche. "Just got in, figured I'd pick up some supplies over at the Art Deco Supermarket and I saw your light was on."

"Come in, please."

Her bed was a mess of covers, pillows and little cushions, it had been eight days since she'd gotten any real rest, didn't even have time to make the bed properly, even worse, the night before the Heat won their playoff game and the Al Capone got slammed. Lucky for her, the bar had a new bar hand to keep her out of the weeds, a young guy, nice so far, named Campero.

"I was gonna order a Domino's pizza, you want?" she asked him.

On top of the tiredness that kept her from routine chores, she'd been consumed reading Lizárraga's *Ciudad Maldita* that had just come out and the *Revólver* guys had thrown a release party for it during a Literatura Callejera night.

"Sure thing, I'll take a slice, or two," he replied. "Lizárraga's book any good?"

"Yeah, I recommend it."

"Okay, I'll buy it."

"I'll get it from Wild Cat at the bar and then you can repay me."

"Sure."

She called the pizza shop, and they sat at the little table to wait for the delivery in front of Lizárraga's book. The copy was pristine, Lizárraga's photo on the back cover, the title in turquoise lettering. Under it, a black and white photo of palm trees swaying in Miami Beach; a hype quote in pink letters announcing it as America's first Tropical Noir written in Spanish.

"Did you read this already?" Karina asked as she got up to grab a basket next to her nightstand that was filled with copies of the New Yorker and *Revólver*, pulling the last of the local magazines dedicated to Lizárraga.

"No, I was at the release at the Al Capone but I didn't get one."

"Take it if you want."

"Cool, thanks, I'll read it before I go to sleep."

There was a knock at the door.

Karina excused herself. The pizza had arrived.

4.

"Please don't smoke, not here anyways," pleaded Officer Pérez.

Comanche had just gotten into the squad car; he didn't have enough time to enjoy a cigarette with his coffee since Pérez had shown up at 7:40 a.m. and not 8 like they had agreed. Major Tito Robalca lived near the hotel, on West Avenue. On the way there, Pérez explained how Robalca's son, Mario, had gone out last Thursday on his way to Miami Dade College and had not come back. At first, the Major and his wife, Lidia, didn't worry, Mario was like any young man – wanted to rule the world and they were used to him leaving one day and returning the next. But this time, it had been three days and no word from him.

"And I take it no one's called asking for ransom money?"

"That's right Comanche, no one."

"And we are absolutely sure this is not a kidnapping?"

"Completely."

"Gimmie five minutes to smoke a cigarette," Comanche asked when Pérez parked in one of the guest spots at Robalca's building – a white, four-story affair with large balconies, blueish doors and windows, with views of West Avenue on one side, and Biscayne Bay on the other.

"You smoke too much, Comanche," said Pérez, emphasizing his dislike by putting some distance between himself and the acrid smoke.

"You know, if I were able to smoke even more, I would," said Comanche, slightly amused, as he dropped the Marlboro on the floor, crushing the butt with the tip of his sole before following Pérez into the building.

Major Tito Robalca was athletic for 56, the Drakkar Noir thick on him, the pastel yellow Tommy Hilfiger polo tucked into navy blue slacks accentuating his musculature. His belt was one of those fancy braided types. They shook hands and went into the living room. Lidia greeted them from a fluffy brown leather loveseat, in front of a small table that had a crystal carafe with water, and a white porcelain kettle filled with coffee.

"Help yourselves," said Robalca, pointing to the table.

They both accepted the offer, their second coffee of the day.

"A little water too?" asked Lidia as she filled their cups.

"Thanks."

"Alright," said Robalca after taking a sip from the cup Lidia had just handed him. "I imagine Officer Pérez has brought you up to speed?"

"I have a few questions," interrupted Comanche before the Major continued.

"Go ahead."

"At what time, exactly, did your son leave on Thursday?"

"Around 7 in the morning."

"I asked Officer Pérez why you're so sure it is not a kidnapping," said Comanche, pausing to sip his coffee. "Can you explain that to me?"

"It's not the first time Mario disappeared but this time it's been a few days with no word from him."

"So, we can rule out a kidnapping…"

"That's right, Comanche."

"Okay, but why hasn't he returned? Did you guys get into a fight? Can we assume he left because of that?"

"That's right," said Robalca nodding his head. "We had an argument, and he left."

"What was the argument about?"

"Money. What we argue about. He always asks for money but does nothing to earn it."

"What's the relationship like between you two and Mario?"

"Like any other, with its ups and downs."

"What's he studying? Do you know his class schedule?"

"Business," interrupted Lidia, "and I have a copy of his schedule."

"Okay, any friends or schoolmates?"

"Not that we *really* know of."

"Here, it's only you two and him?"

"Yes, Mario is an only child."

"Any neighbors or anyone in the neighborhood who might've seen him go out at that time on Thursday?"

"Tula saw him, our cleaning lady."

"What did she say?"

"Nothing, that he said goodbye at the door."

"How does he get to school?"

"He takes the bus because parking at the College is impossible. He has a car, there," said Robalca, standing up to point out a sporty black Honda Civic in the lot.

"Drugs? Alcohol?"

"He's like any teenager," replied Robalca.

"Sorry Major, but that reply tells me nothing," said Comanche. "I'm asking you directly if Mario drinks or uses drugs."

"Well," sighed Lidia, "he's had some issues but nothing too crazy."

"Issues? How so?" asked Comanche, taking another sip from the coffee that had cooled down to an agreeable temperature.

"Drugs and alcohol," Robalca said, not hiding a growing disdain towards Comanche.

"Does he have a girlfriend? Boyfriend?"

"*Marito* is straight," said Lidia, raising her voice. "And he doesn't have a girlfriend at the moment."

"What about Tula? Can I speak with her?"

"Of course," replied Lidia. "She should be here any moment now."

"What time to what time does she work?"

"She usually comes in around this time and leaves in the afternoon, around 4, after she takes the dog out for a walk at the park."

"Can I have a look in his room while we wait?"

Mario Robalca's room was sparse, only a twin bed against a wall. No nightstand or desk. The closet had a few shirts and jeans, the latter yielding nothing after Comanche searched the pockets. He looked under the bed too: nothing. What caught his eyes were a pair of black Everlast boxing gloves hanging from a nail on the wall, next to a photo of Muhammad Ali, including the famous one with the Beatles on Miami Beach when he used to train in the 5th Street Gym with Angelo Dundee. Comanche had no clue where the legendary boxing gym used to be.

"Your son is a fighter? He boxes?"

"A little," Robalca said. "Sometimes he leaves the house with his pair of gloves."

"Does he go to any local boxing gym?"

"No, no," said Robalca. "It's more like a hobby for him."

"He idolizes Muhammad Ali," said Lidia. "Ever since he was a little boy."

"I'm going to need a copy of that class schedule," Comanche said. "And a photo."

"I'll get those for you," said Lidia.

"Let's go back to the living room," said Robalca, motioning Comanche and Pérez out of the room.

In the living room, an awkward silence grew between the men, broken by the Major as he – hands firmly inside his pockets – whistled the melody to *"Tropecé de nuevo y con la misma piedra"* pacing in front of his bar filled with single malt bottles. The doorbell rang. It was Tula.

"Any clue where Mario could be?" Comanche asked, catching the woman off-guard.

"This gentleman is helping us find him," said Robalca, quickly to put her at ease.

"No, sir," replied Tula.

"When's the last time you saw him?" Comanche asked.

"The last day he was here, sir."

"Notice anything different about him?"

"No, sir."

"I'm not talking about that day only, I mean if anything seemed off the last couple of weeks, was he behaving differently in any way?"

"No, sir."

"Okay, you can go on with your day, we're done for now," said Comanche.

Lidia returned with a photo of Mario Robalca and a copy of the class schedule folded in fourths. Comanche took one last sip of coffee and thanked the couple for the cup and their time.

Before getting in the squad car, he asked Pérez for five minutes so he could smoke, hanging his Ray-Ban aviators on his shirt collar.

"Fine," the officer said, "what do you think so far?"

"I'm gonna say that if Major Tito Robalca wants to keep this as quiet as possible, I'm going to assume the 'minor' issues with drugs and alcohol translate to the kid being a junkie or an alcoholic."

"I agree with you, and I appreciate you having that talk with them, you know, bringing that up," said Pérez. "He's my C.O., I didn't know how to broach this comfortably."

"No girlfriend, apparently no friends."

Major Tito Robalca was tight-lipped given what an upstanding citizen the boy must be was Comanche's take.

"Could be," said Pérez. "Where do you want to start with this, any clue?"

"There's also the possibility that he's already dead."

"Let's hope not, but yeah, there is."

"And the Major, he's off today?" Comanche asked, trying to add a bit of irony to his comment. "I mean, those weren't work clothes."

"He's on vacation leave, everyone thinks he's got family

from out of town. Only I know that it's about the kid. His head's not into work now, can't blame the guy."

"I'm going to need all of your help on this."

"Whatever you say, Comanche."

"Get a list of all the local boxing gyms and have one of your guys inquire after the kid at all of them."

"That's not a bit much?"

"No, and I have something else in mind that I'll prioritize."

"What's that?"

"You know Ilusiones?" asked Comanche as he fastened the seatbelt in the squad car's passenger's seat.

"That café?"

"Yeah, drop me off there and wait for my call," said Comanche, suspecting the Major had held back on what he'd told them.

5.

"Oh shit, look who it is!" exclaimed Consorte. "Who else but *the* Comanche of all Comanches!"

"One and the same, fucker."

"Extra pepper?"

"And get me some Cuban toasts drowned in butter."

"Sure thing bro, but first tell me what brings you around these parts?"

Comanche put Mario Robalca's photo on the counter, letting Consorte know that he'd have to speak with Chamizo since he, too, was a business student over at Miami Dade College and that it was a missing person's case, the son of a high-ranking cop.

"You call him, the fuck I look like to you?" replied Consorte. "You see a skirt? Shaved legs? You sayin' I'm your secretary?"

"No asshole, no one asked you to," said Comanche who had already texted Chamizo on his way to El Ilusiones. Instead of arguing, he asked Consorte to get his breakfast going. In the meantime, he'd sink a couple of balls while he waited.

He lit a Marlboro, asked for some Héctor Lavoe on the hi-fi, and to the sounds of *"El Todopoderoso,"* he got lost in the infinite possibilities of the green felt and its numerous cancerous pockmarks. Comanche had never been interested in driving, never even wanted a car. The only real luxury he'd ever awarded himself had been a German, cinnamon brown balsa wood cue. It was so smooth that it slipped effortlessly through the dip of the knuckle between his index and middle fingers like the finest silk. He'd bought it from El Pelao, one of the real pool sharks from the Palacio Hall – the same man who'd taught him everything about the game. El Pelao needed some quick cash to get the Lada he worked as a taxi straightened out. One of the headlights was out, the starter wonky, and the scarce Russian replacement parts he could find had gotten more expensive. He'd gotten a ticket from the cops; he couldn't operate a taxi that way.

"A thousand for the stick," El Pelao had offered. "You know it cost me three times that." Comanche only had $800, he was barely legal and had only been going to the Palacio since he was 14, saving all the money he'd won betting. He didn't have a single cent more. El Pelao had no choice, leaving the cue on the table, he'd be able to get the light and starter fixed, maybe even have some left over for a few cases of beer.

"What's up, *papi*? said Chamizo as Comanche worked his aim on the white ball.

"Two twenties," replied Comanche.

"No, *marico*, I'm fucking broke," said Chamizo, who'd spent the last dollar of his last paycheck the night before on pitchers and wings while watching the Heat game with friends.

"Fine, easy," Comanche said. "I just wanna talk about something else anyway."

"Let's sit at the bar, what you drinking?"

"Coke."

Consorte served Comanche's peppery fried eggs and Cuban toast on the counter and a Coca-Cola with a glass full of ice cubes for Chamizo.

"Start talking, *papi*; I'm curious about this."

"You know him?" asked Comanche showing him Mario's photo.

"Let me see?" said Chamizo, pulling the photo closer to himself. "No, *mi pana*, I don't know who that is."

"Business student at Miami Dade, I thought maybe you'd crossed paths."

"No man, there's thousands of students, dozens of class schedules."

"Okay, what about this then?" he pulled the class schedule from his pocket. "Can you help me figure this out?"

"Uh, a class schedule."

"Yeah."

"What do you want to figure out?" said Chamizo with a chuckle.

"What the fuck these codes and abbreviations mean."

"Well, for starters, he's got Intro to Computer Science in classroom 2B, that's building 2, see? At 3 p.m. with Professor Ramírez today."

"Okay, you mind going with me to the college at that time?"

"Sure, I'm on campus at that time. I'll walk you to the room if you want."

"How's everything over here?" asked Consorte, looking at Comanche's empty plate.

"You got any croquetas left?"

"Of course."

"Get one for him too, I don't like to eat with people who are not eating."

"Thanks, *pana*."

"Game?"

"Twenty a game like I said?"

"Sure."

"Okay, you're on."

6.

Miami Dade College was an ocean of youngsters barely out of high school, uniformed in Converse high tops, their noses burrowed into cellphone screens, the ravages of acne disappearing into adulthood. Chamizo led Comanche through the urban, downtown campus to Mario's classroom. Before parting, they agreed on meeting up at the Ilusiones in the coming days for a rematch.

"Panita," said Chamizo after he took a few steps away on his way to the elevators.

"What?"

"You can't do that here," pointing to the pack of Marlboros Comanche had taken out of his pocket.

Comanche stood by the door for a full ten minutes, reclining against the windowless wall illuminated by overhead fluorescents that reminded him of the lighting at the county morgue.

"Professor Ramírez?" asked Comanche, moving into the path of a middle-aged man with an over-the-shoulder book bag who was holding folders and various papers under his arm.

"Yes?"

Comanche showed him his ID and introduced himself, explaining that he was looking for Mario Robalca since he'd left his house early last Thursday and had not returned.

"Robalca?"

"That's right."

Mario Robalca had not been to class for over a month, the professor had already issued a warning that he'd be dropped from the course, but the kid had not replied.

"Give me a second, maybe one of his classmates can help you."

"Please."

Ramírez poked his head into the classroom and motioned for a student to come over.

"Yes, professor?"

"This gentleman," Ramírez said, "is looking for your project partner."

"Oof, Doc, I already told you, it's like the earth swallowed him. He hasn't done any of the assignments and I haven't heard from him. I've done all the work."

"What's your name?" Comanche interrupted.

"My name is Brandon García."

"Okay, Brandon," said Comanche showing him his ID. "Mario Robalca's been missing since last Thursday and I would greatly appreciate it if you could tell me anything you can remember that might help me find him."

Brandon García and Mario Robalca had been in a pair of classes together before, that was it. In this Intro to Computer Science course, Professor Ramírez had paired them up on a project, but García had done all the work and had given up trying to get Mario to do his part. He could see in the texts that Robalca had read them, but he never replied.

"When's the last time you wrote to him?"

"Over a week ago," showing Comanche his phone to prove it.

"May I?" Comanche asked, enlarging Robalca's profile picture – it was the same photo of Muhammad Ali that he had on the wall next to his bed. "Can I give you my number and you contact me if he ever responds?"

"Sure, no problem."

"That's it," said Comanche. "Thank you, Brandon, and Professor Ramírez."

"If you speak to him," Brandon said. "Tell him he's getting an F cuz he's done nothing."

7.

Comanche wanted to sit down with Tula again and ask her more questions about Mario. He wasn't done with their conversation, but he knew that if the kid was up to his balls in drugs and was fucking up, she wouldn't have said anything in front of Major Tito Robalca and his wife. Who did Mario hang out with? Who did he go out with? At what time? That sort of thing. He'd been sitting for half an hour on a bench at the Maurice Gibb Park behind the Robalca's building, waiting for Tula to walk the dog, one of her last duties for the day as he'd been told. Cigarette after cigarette, his Ray-Ban aviators on, the afternoon was an idyllic postcard of sailboats moored between the condos of Biscayne Boulevard and the mansions on the Venetian Causeway. Finally, Tula, in her uniform and espadrilles, came out of the building, a cocker spaniel dragging behind her on a little red leash.

"Excuse me… Tula?" said Comanche, opting for timid politeness before putting the screws to her. "I need a couple minutes of your time, if you don't mind."

"Sir?"

Comanche noted her Andean features and the birthmark on her left cheek. It was the size of a roach.

"Can we?"

"Didn't we speak the other day?"

"I'd rather not make this a formal interrogation at the station; depends entirely on you."

Tula del Águila was hired two years prior by the Robalcas, and in the time since, had barely spoken to Mario. Every time they crossed paths, and she greeted him, the boy lowered his eyes. Lately, almost every week, some dudes in a tinted car with a loud muffler, came by. Each time, one of the guys, a fat dude with a ponytail would get into loud arguments with him. One time it even came to blows and the Major had come outside, armed, to scare them away.

"Wait a minute, Tula," said Comanche, "what color is the car?"

"It's dark."

"Dark, yeah, but like what? Black? Blue? Green?"

"Yes."

"Yes, what? Tell me what the car and the fat guy look like."

"I already told you sir, the car is dark, tinted windows, music always blasting, and the muffler makes infernal noises. One time they came in a white car and another time in a red car."

"And the fat guy?"

"Tufo, leave him alone!" The dog peed on some bushes and sniffed Comanche's shoes.

"Keep going."

"Yes, sorry, he's fat and has long hair, wears his pants low, you can see his butt. He looks like he eats Big Macs all day and plays PlayStation for a living."

"When's the last time you saw them?"

"Tufo! Stop it!" Tula scolded the dog. "Not long ago. Last week I think… let me see… Wednesday, yes, last Wednesday."

"Around what time?"

"Around this time. The same time I bring Tufo out for his number twos."

"Thanks, that's all I need."

"Okay sir, at your service."

"Thanks."

"And another thing."

"Yes?"

"The boy went out many times for walks down Alton Road with his boxing gloves."

"Down Alton?"

"Yes sir, with his gloves slung over his shoulder, down that way, towards South Pointe."

"Okay."

The cocker spaniel barked until Comanche was well out of sight.

Comanche would have to organize this puzzle in his head. Mario Robalca associated with some dudes in a particular kind of car and the first thing that came to mind was the dudes who'd been looking for Luigi Lechuga in a blue Mitsubishi at Joe's on the Venetian. But that didn't mean anything: everybody in Miami had a car so it didn't mean these were the same guys. On the other hand, Tula was very clear about a fat guy in the group, something Roy Morris had never said about the crew after Lechuga. Best thing to do was find the car she described. Then there was the bit about the gloves and Mario's fascination with boxing that – according to his dad – was not a sport he practiced. And yet, here he had an eyewitness who'd seen him leave the house with the gloves. If he wasn't training, then what the fuck was he doing walking around with them? Ridiculous. If he wasn't a member of any of the local gyms and all he wanted was to shadowbox for exercise, why wouldn't he do it at the Maurice Gibb Park right behind his home?

"Comanche," answered Pérez on the first ring.

"We have something," said Comanche, lighting up a Marlboro. "But we have to move quickly on it."

"I'm listening."

"Mario Robalca has not been to school in a while, and he's involved with some thugs in a car who've been to his home. The Major knows all about it too."

"Okay."

"This car, Officer," Comanche said. "We need to find it."

"Right, right, but how?"

"They've met at Maurice Gibb Park and all the parks on the Beach have security cameras. Last Wednesday they came for him, around this time."

"You said Maurice Gibb?"

"Yup."

"Okay, first thing tomorrow in the morning," said Pérez. "My CCTV guy is off today."

"Off? You don't have a backup?"

"No."

"Fuck."

"Yeah, we're fucked. Budgets."

There could be a plan B, but according to Comanche, it was a bit far-fetched. The people Luigi Lechuga owed money to were collecting at Joe's on the Venetian in a blue car. A blue Mitsubishi. Comanche wasn't sure if those looking for Robalca had a blue car since Tula had mentioned they came once in a white car and another time in a red one. But it was the same kind of vehicle, the same pattern, so they could be related. Comanche could talk to Roy Morris, the owner of Joe's, and check the cameras for the Mitsubishi, which would take long hours and cross-check to see if they were the same crooks.

"I don't know, Comanche," said Pérez. "That's a weak link."

Comanche agreed but if they waited for the video surveillance officer to return, they'd lose a full day. Without access to the CCTV footage, there was nothing they could do.

"Well, forge on."

"Fine, I'll go by and speak with Roy Morris in the meantime."

Before he hung up, Comanche asked Pérez if his men had finished canvassing the boxing gyms. Nothing had turned up since there was only one gym on Alton and he'd sent one of his best, Sergio Barboza, a young Salvadorean hungry to rise through the ranks, to interview the front desk clerk. No one had seen Mario there.

"Text me the name and address."

"What's the matter, Comanche? Don't trust my guy?"

"No, no, it's not that," Comanche said, explaining that both the Major and his wife had seen the kid leave with boxing gloves, and another one of his sources had said the same, and he was worried the clerk might've been intimidated by a uniformed officer.

"Well then, just sent it."

The walk to Joe's took 20 minutes, but Comanche hardly noticed amidst the sea of cyclists, rollerbladers, and people out for walks that was Miami Beach at that time of the afternoon. It was early, so Comanche knocked on the doors of the darkened bar, figuring either Roy Morris or Caroline, the bartender, would answer. Nothing. He knocked again, harder this time, and waited. Still nothing. He walked to the back, to the alleyway where he had caught Luigi Lechuga before. A little farther down, a bald guy with a large gut was taking heavy drags on a cigarette behind the Mykonos restaurant. He told Comanche Joe's closed at least a month ago after the owner suffered a massive coronary. He had no clue if the guy was dead or alive.

"You need something?"

"Yes," said Comanche, showing his ID.

The bald guy introduced himself, Kostas Jaritos, owner of the Mykonos for the last ten years. He rolled his R's, really dragging the letter out in every word, wore nice leather shoes and a white shirt that had the nasty, mustard yellow rings of sweat around his armpits no amount of bleach would ever clear up. Mykonos closed around the time people started coming into Joe's, and Kostas hardly came out back for a smoke since he had smoked in his office. Everything Comanche was telling him was news to him.

"What about that?" Comanche pointed to a security camera perched above the restaurant's door.

"It's fixed at an angle, doesn't catch movement much farther from here."

"Well, Mr. Jaritos, thank you for your time, I appreciate it."

Comanche turned the corner and took out his phone to call Pérez. Dead end with Morris, the bar had been closed for over a month.

"Joe's on the Venetian?"

"Yeah, the owner had a heart attack, and I don't know if he's dead, but the place closed after that."

"Shit, news to me. Well then, I guess tomorrow morning it is."

"Yes."

The night was just starting, and the best way to end the day would be at the Al Capone. Their two-for-one cocktails during Happy Hour were good, but better still would be Karina's firm ass in her tight black pants.

Comanche had the bar to himself, save for a couple sharing a basket of chicken wings and a pitcher of Michelob. In the background, the house speakers had The Smiths' "Bigmouth Strikes Again" playing at an agreeable volume.

"Weird seeing you here so early," Karina said.

"Closed up shop for the day."

"You beat the rush. Gonna get slammed when the Heat start playing."

"Had no clue they were playing."

"Of course, the Playoffs," she said. Cabalito had texted

her that he'd be coming by with the Chismosa staff, and she thought the *Revólver* guys would pass by too.

"Okay."

"Rum?" she asked, placing an ashtray and a coaster with Al Capone's caricature drawn in grey ink before him.

"Fully loaded," he said, motioning with his fingers how much of the spirit he wanted in his glass. The electric shock that zapped through his cock when she turned and bent down to grab a clean glass didn't exactly take him by surprise.

8.

Comanche turned on the coffee maker and added two scoops of Bustelo before he turned on the hot water tap in the shower. Sitting on the toilet, he thought of how pleasant it would be to come out of a steamy shower and be greeted by the delicious aroma.

He left the bathroom door open.

"Good morning," said Mariolys on the phone. "I'm in a rush, so I'm putting you on speaker." It was her second day at El Dolarazo in the Mall of the Americas. She wanted to be on time. Her first day had gone very well with the owner, Iñaki, commending her for straightening out the shelves – bookmarkers with photos of the Egyptian pyramids were haphazardly thrown in with colanders, colanders mixed up in the bin with cinnamon gum boxes, assorted chewing gums with the Hello Kitty keychains, and so on. The place had been a fucking mess.

"What time you go in?"

"At nine, but the jitney takes forever."

Mariolys had insisted on the one-bedroom on Flagler near the mall and Romero's agency. It was convenient for them both. But she worried if they didn't jump on it, it'd be rented out to someone else. She wanted to pay the deposit and move in as soon as he got back from the Beach.

"What they ask, first and last?"

"Just one month, nothing else."

"Okay."

"I'll go today, right when I'm done at El Dolarazo."

Comanche enjoyed his Sundays. On his bed, wearing nothing but his underwear, eating takeout *pan con bistec* from La Carreta and wiping the mustard off on the sheets.

He liked taking a shit with the bathroom door open and getting fucked up at night at the Aruba with his friend, the barkeep, Tony el Vasco, who always hooked him up with a bag of coke and a nod and a wink towards whatever woman at the bar had just broken up, was trashed, or was just looking for a quickie. But soon, even though Mariolys kept him company, fucked his brains out, and accepted him for who he was, flaws and all, he'd be putting an end to his old ways. Even when he told her that he didn't want kids, his only demand, she agreed and was cool with it.

He checked the time on his phone, it was still early. He lit a Marlboro and opened up the latest *Revólver* on Wild Cat's article dedicated to Lizárraga.

By Wild Cat

In memory of Maxi Lizárraga

Charles Willeford's Shadow

One of the authors who has most influenced all contemporary local noir genre writers is Charles Willeford.

The brief literary history of Miami is no more than 60 or 70 years old, although it was only in the 1980s that it began to take the paths that characterize it today: the noir genre and stories about cultural clashes. In 1985, **Continental Drift** by Russell Banks appeared, a work that, without exaggeration, can be considered 'the great Miami novel,' and in 1987, in the realm of nonfiction, T.D. Allman released **Miami, City of the**

Future, perhaps the most relevant book for understanding the city. However, the turning point in Miami's literary trajectory came between 1984 and 1988 with Charles Willeford, when he published the Hoke Moseley detective novels, which include **Miami Blues** (1984), **New Hope for the Dead** (1985), **Sideswipe** (1987), and **The Way We Die Now** (1988).

Like many Miamians, Willeford wasn't born in Miami; he arrived in the 1960s at the age of 41 after a journey through other U.S. cities, France, and Peru. He studied English Literature at the University of Miami, and later taught at Miami Dade College.

Despite having nearly 20 titles to his name, he didn't enjoy significant literary recognition until the Hoke Moseley saga appeared, set in the grimy streets of Miami during the notorious 1980s. Moseley, divorced and a heavy drinker, lived in a Miami Beach hostel and worked as a gritty street cop. His world was populated by Mexicans, Cubans, gang members, drug traffickers, and undocumented Haitians. However, the value of these works, beyond their literary quality, lies in the fact that the detective, in each episode, discovered and confronted Latin American culture and a city he never fully understood but had to accept to adapt to his surroundings. Even in his workplace, more and more of his colleagues appeared with last names like Pérez and Sánchez, including his patrol partner Ellita, a Cuban woman whom he initially viewed with disdain but later becomes his roommate.

Without a doubt, Miami left a mark on Willeford, and through Hoke Moseley, he pulled back the curtain on a city that was previously little known, bearing no resemblance to the image it projected. That has changed little: our narrators—whether the more commercial ones writing in English, like Carl Hiaasen or Les Standiford, or the more indie authors writing in Spanish, like those from **Viaje One Way: Antología de narradores de Miami**—recreate the city, sometimes in a noir tone, other times highlighting cultural friction, but in both cases, portraying it as hostile and hard to understand. They, too, reveal a very different city than the one people think they know.

Willeford died of a heart attack in 1988, without knowing that he was laying the first strokes of the literary identity of a city that, 25 years later, is still not fully consolidated but is on its way. The fifth book of the Moseley saga was never published: it remains a manuscript. **Miami Blues** was adapted into a film in 1990, and although it wasn't a huge success, it is considered one of Miami's classic films.

To call Willeford the father of Miami literature might be too ambitious, but it is fair to say that the shadow of Charles Willeford lingers among the pages of our authors.

REVÓLVER
EDICIONES

Revólver Ediciones is a publication by undocumented writers and journalists clandestinely operating within Miami Beach.

9.

"Any news?" asked Major Tito Robalca, standing under the entrance door, both hands in his pockets. "I wasn't expecting you back so soon."

"We need to talk, clearly."

"I don't understand, Comanche."

"You're holding back."

The Major lowered his gaze and fidgeted, then, in a lower tone, he asked Comanche to follow him a little farther into the apartment. He didn't want to bother Lidia; her nerves were frayed, and she was teetering on a full-blown meltdown. Yes, it was true, he had failed to mention the guys in the cars who'd been looking for Mario. He'd tried talking to the boy, but it ended up in an argument that went nowhere.

"Mister Robalca," Comanche said, "did you know your son gambles?"

"Like cards? A gambling addiction?"

"Yes."

"Not that I know of, why do you ask?"

"I'm following some clues that are pointing towards that."

"How so?"

"The guys who came around," Comanche said, "if I'm right, are involved in that."

"Oh."

"When's the last time you saw them around here?"

"Last week, Wednesday. They came around the back of the building, the side overlooking the bay."

"What car was it?"

"A black Jetta, they don't always come in the same car."

"How many of them."

"Two? Three? I don't know," Robalca said. "What I do know is they were hoodlums." He particularly did not like the fat guy who usually sat in the passenger seat. That son of a bitch would get out of the car and start yelling in the middle of the street. One time he had to come out and discharge his piece in the air to run them off.

"You get a license plate number?"

"No, Comanche. I never wanted this to become a thing, but I think I fucked up."

"I think the same," Comanche said, pulling out his cigarettes and offering the Major one before putting one in his lips.

"Quit a year ago. How did you know about them? What've you found out?"

"I'd rather not say yet."

"There's something else," Robalca said. "At the time, Lidia and I turned a blind eye but now that you mention the gambling, it's important."

"What?"

"A few times, some of our valuables went missing. Some of Lidia's jewelry, a Cartier watch, and the last was a silverware set my wife inherited from her mother that had been brought here from Cuba. It was the only thing she brought with her when they fled Cuba in the sixties on a small propeller plane that crossed the straight and landed in the Opa-Locka airport. It's what I confronted him about on Wednesday. That's what we fought about."

"What did you do about it?"

"How so?"

"Things went missing. Missing. That's theft. What did you and your wife do about it?"

"We couldn't prove it was him," the Major said, looking away. They had fired their maids, three different ones during the thefts, but all three had mentioned seeing Mario go out with those guys. He and his wife had decided to keep it under wraps.

"Well, Major, it seems like we're speaking more clearly with each other now," said Comanche. "Why did you hold back before?"

"I wasn't comfortable saying all this in front of Pérez, but I figured you'd come back anyways, and you did."

"I gotta go."

"Keep me posted."

Comanche made his way to the Miami Beach Police Department. As he crossed Lincoln Road and Washington Avenue, where he could see the façade of boarded windows and the smog-shadowed ghost of the sign that promised 'Chicas Latinas' on what had been Casa de Muñecas, his phone rang.

"Comanche."

"Please tell me you have the footage from the Maurice Gibb Park."

"That and more."

"Be there in half an hour."

"I'll be waiting for you," said Officer Pérez.

10.

The walls of the Knockout Gym were covered in mirrors, making the place look much bigger than it was, but it couldn't hide that it was small, had a few speed bags and heavy bags, and the ring dominated much of the floor.

"This guy box in here?" asked Comanche, placing Mario's photo and his ID on the Knockout Gym's front desk. "I'm looking for him."

The clerk excused himself, said he was new, and that if he remembered correctly, the cops had been by asking for the man in the photo too, but at the time, he'd been helping a pair of new members enroll and was trying to explain he'd only been there a week.

"Who can help me then?"

"Percy!" said the clerk over the loudspeaker, looking towards the back of the gym where several guys sparred; the crackle on the system momentarily interrupting Europe's "The Final Countdown."

Comanche stopped Percy, a young man with a bare, muscular, sweaty torso, wearing boots and boxing gloves, before the clerk could explain why calling him over. Percy didn't pay much attention to the photo of Mario Robalca. Yes, of course, he knew him—at Knockout Gym, they called him "The Crazy One." He always walked by the door, heading down Alton Road, never looking up, with his boxing gloves slung over his shoulder, and that caught their attention, especially since they usually chatted outside after training. Once, one of the guys, Jarocho, tried to talk to him, to invite him to train.

"Quite the coincidence for a boxer to walk by a boxing gym and not exchange a word with the boxers, don't you think? But The Crazy One didn't even lift his eyes from the ground."

"Other than that, any other contact with him?"

"No, to be honest, no."

"How often did he walk by, would you say?"

"Shit, like three or four times a week, maybe more."

"Remember when the last time was?"

"Last Friday, early," said Percy without skipping a beat. That was the last day he'd been at the gym since he went to Peru the following day to visit family over the weekend. He'd just returned the previous evening and was certain it had been Friday.

"And he was walking down Alton, I suppose?"

"That's right."

"Did you notice if he was carrying a bag or anything like that?" asked Comanche, thinking that if Mario Robalca had left home, logically, he would've grabbed some clothes.

"No sir," said Percy. "Truth is, I didn't really notice. I

just thought the Muhammad Ali t-shirt he had on was pretty cool."

"Thanks, Percy, that'll do," said Comanche, stretching his hand out to shake his.

11.

Officer Pérez waited for Comanche at his office with Barboza. His desk was covered with prints from video surveillance. Some of a black Jetta like Major Tito Robalca had said, others of the fat guy with the long hair: Franko Battiri. Battiri was known to them as a loan shark who always held valuables as collateral. He'd been taken in before for extorsion, but they could never build a strong case. His front was a body shop on Purdy where he rebuilt antique cars and sold them to collectors or rich Russians or Brazilians who lived on Fisher Island.

"Let's go to his shop," said Comanche.

"That's why he's here," said Officer Pérez, motioning

to Sergio Barboza. The plan was that Comanche and Barboza would be taken there by Pérez and the officer would wait for them outside in the squad car while they interviewed Battiri.

"Okay," Comanche said, "but there's one more thing."

"What's that?"

Without telling them he'd been by the Knockout Gym to not give away he'd been following up on Barboza's investigations there, he told them that one of his informants mentioned seeing Mario Robalca walking down Alton with his boxing gloves slung over his shoulders. And that was the last time he'd been seen.

"What do you propose?"

"Get a unit in that area. There's a chance he's hiding out around there."

"You know I can't let this get any bigger than it is," Pérez said. "We have to keep this contained amongst us." Sergio Barboza would check the area Comanche suggested, and he and Comanche would go to Battiri's, with Comanche engaging the long haired hood – but they'd have to do it in a couple of hours because Barboza was scheduled to lift fingerprints at a 7-Eleven on Washington, where two men, one Latino and the other Anglo, brutally beat a Black guy with a baseball bat, leaving him fighting for his life in an emergency room bed.

12.

Comanche sat at the bar in the Ilusiones, lit a Marlboro, and ordered eggs, as usual.

"You gonna make me work? *Cojones!*" exclaimed Consorte. He wasn't moving. Papito had invited him to a cookout the night before to watch the Heat game, and the night got longer with each passing bottle of Grey Goose, Johnnie Walker, Patrón, young girls, and a glass-topped table that was zigzagged by copious lines of coke.

"Why do you try to hang with the adults?"

"Bro, Papito's cookouts are great," replied Consorte. "Did you watch the game?"

"No." He'd gone by the Al Capone to square up with Karina for some drinks.

"Dumbass," said Consorte, adding Papito wanted to thank Comanche for getting Runcho and Gitano taken care of. He owed him – whatever he wanted, all he had to do was ask.

"Right, you wouldn't know if there'd been an article on the Bee Gees in Miami Beach in an old copy of *Revólver?*" said Comanche, trying to change the subject.

"Yeah, I think so, I've got it here somewhere," Consorte said. "They wrote it up about Maurice Gibb Park."

Comanche needed the Glock, dealing with hoods like Franko Battiri required it. Consorte would grab that after he finished frying his eggs. Comanche picked up the issue of *Revólver* that Consorte put on the bar when his text alerts went off. Karina had his copy of *Ciudad Maldita* at her place if he wanted to grab it. He thanked her and texted he'd be by in a bit.

By Wild Cat

The Bee Gees' American Dream

Right when it seemed like it was time for the Bee
Gees to call it quits, an ace up their sleeve appeared:
Miami Beach

On March 4th, 2007, a ceremony was held in a small park
in Miami Beach, on Purdy Avenue, overlooking the Venetian
Causeway and the open waters of Biscayne Bay. Until then,
the park had been named Island View Park, but from that
day on, it would be renamed Maurice Gibb Memorial Park.
Three years earlier, Maurice had not survived surgery for

an intestinal blockage that had sent him to Mount Sinai Hospital.

The Gibb brothers made a pact from a very young age, which was to become one of the biggest music bands in the world. Born in the United Kingdom, they emigrated to Australia when Barry, the eldest, was 13, and the twins Maurice and Robin were eight. Soon, they began their musical adventures at school and with friends, then on stages and on television shows. Their album **The Bee Gees Sing and Play 14 Barry Gibb Songs** was released in 1965. Although they achieved a period of glory, Australia is neither Europe nor the United States, and they had already reached the ceiling there.

The Bee Gees returned to England in the late sixties, where Robert Stigwood, partner of The Beatles' manager Brian Epstein, was waiting for them with high expectations and a contract that only needed their signatures. At first, the public was not indifferent, but they didn't reach the expected level of success either. In one of their performances, they were even pelted with eggs. At that time, the UK was the realm of The Beatles, and if The Bee Gees wanted to rise, they needed to move closer to that style, both musically and lyrically, and move away from love ballads. The group considered the idea of breaking up, among other things, but their friend Eric Clapton suggested they try their luck in America. Miami, Florida to be exact. Clapton had secluded himself in Miami Beach, recovering from his heroin addiction, in a house at 461 Ocean Boulevard, near the Criteria Studios, where he recorded "Layla" and was preparing his next album, which would be titled after the house's address, with the photo on the cover.

The Gibb brothers landed in Miami Beach, spending some time at 461 Ocean Boulevard and, with the help of producer Arif Mardin, seeking a transformation at Criteria Studios, which at that time was a small mecca for musicians, where Bob Dylan, The Eagles, Bob Marley, Fleetwood Mac, and James Brown had recorded for Atlantic Records. The Bee

Gees' first single in Miami, "Jive Talkin'," was born in the van that took them down Biscayne Boulevard from Ocean Boulevard to Criteria, and it revealed a new side of them, one with rock rhythms, earning them top spots on the Billboard charts. The release of the album **Main Course**, featuring the songs "Winds of Change," "Fanny," and "Nights on Broadway," confirmed the quality of their new work and marked the change they had long sought. Later, the soundtrack for **Saturday Night Fever** would follow, cementing The Bee Gees' recognition as the greatest disco band in history.

In addition to **Main Course**, The Bee Gees recorded the albums **E.S.P.** and **Spirits Having Flown at Criteria**, considered by many critics to be their best work, featuring the songs "Tragedy" and "Too Much Heaven," which took them to the top of the charts not only in the United States but also in the United Kingdom. By the late seventies and early eighties, the Gibb family had already settled in Miami Beach, and in some interviews, when asked why they chose to live in this city, the answer was that Miami, and its climate had captivated them from day one.

REVÓLVER
EDICIONES

Revólver Ediciones is a publication by undocumented writers and journalists clandestinely operating within Miami Beach.

13.

"Sorry for the mess," said Karina, excusing the appearance of her efficiency that greeted Comanche in the same disarray each time he'd been there before.

"No worries," Comanche said, hanging his Ray-Bans on his shirt collar.

"I was gonna wash my clothes, but haven't had a chance," she said, looking down at the hamper, "the bar was crazy busy yesterday."

"Cuz of the Heat?"

"Yeah, you didn't stay, right? Cabalito showed up with Peru and his new girlfriend, a new chick that's working at the taqueria. The *Revólver* guys too. They all asked for you and I said you were around, but I didn't see you anymore."

"Right, place was packed, I don't like it when it gets too full."

"Packed is perfect for me. More people, more tips."

"I guess."

"Would you like a seat?"

Comanche had been standing next to the table with the little red chairs.

"Thanks."

"Coffee?"

"That would be great," said Comanche, taking his Marlboros out.

Karina put on a playlist of Calamaro's songs. "Flaca" came on. She was standing in front of her small oven, working the coffeemaker and Comanche had an unrestricted view of her ass. It wasn't the same as it had been at the bar with the tight pants. Now her baggy Adidas sweats even covered her feet but just the same, he felt that sharp electric burst run down his cock.

"Black, without sugar, right?"

"Ready to mainline," he said, noticing his phone vibrating with Mariolys' number flashing on the screen. He slid the answer button to the red X to decline the call. Karina brought the coffee mugs to the table and then grabbed a dirty glass for Comanche to use as an ashtray and his copy of *Ciudad Maldita*.

"How much do I owe you?"

"Don't worry about it," she said as she added two packets of Splenda and a splash of milk in hers.

"Thank you," Comanche said, thumbing through the book.

A photo fell out and he handed it to her.

"Ah," she said smiling.

It was her brother Fede's birthday today and she called him to wish him well, and it made her feel down. She looked at photos she had stored in a box in her closet, and that one ended up outside. She didn't know how it wound up in Lizárraga's book. The ones in the photo were her, Fede, and her mom, from 10 years ago, at the Ezeiza Airport in front of the International Departures sign, the day she left. None of them had ever left the country, and the excitement and sadness of leaving with no return were like wires crossing and sparking memories of her childhood, when at school, a classmate would return from vacation with a t-shirt that said 'Welcome to Miami' in hot pink letters. Karina would ask her mom to take her to Disney, and her mom would laugh and say, 'That's for rich people, girl.' Maybe for her fifteenth birthday, if they found a cheap little hotel—though the gringos made everything so expensive—they'd go. But at home, they were always scraping by; they got to the end of the month with what her mom earned as a receptionist at the Villanueva Notary's Office, and mending pants and shirts for lawyers, notaries, and the firm's clients.

"And where are you from? I just realized I've never asked."

His text alert came on. It was Mariolys, full of happy faces, heart and red lip emojis to let him know she had paid for the apartment on Flagler. She couldn't wait to celebrate with him and some fiestas. That same afternoon she'd go to K-Mart and Walmart with her cousin Luz to buy sheets, towels, and a bedcover she'd seen before that she liked.

The phone vibrated again; it was Pérez. Comanche excused himself from the room to answer it.

"Comanche."

"Officer, it's been two hours," said Comanche even though it had been between four and five since he had left the Miami Beach Police Department. "We going to Battiri's?"

"Better than that, Comanche, better than that, we got him."

To save time, Pérez changed plans, and he personally took the fingerprints at the 7-Eleven, sending Barboza to follow up on Comanche's intel. Barboza scouted the perimeter for a long four hours, which is why the wait was delayed, but he eventually spotted Robalca getting out of a white Hyundai with four friends and a woman, entering what looked like an abandoned house. It was impossible that the earth had swallowed up that kid, damn it, especially in South Beach, which was a small Hell where everyone got burned together.

"You got him with you?"

"No, I'd like to hit the spot with you. You and Barboza while I wait outside. Pérez did not want the young Robalca to see him and be tipped off to his dad's involvement.

"On my way, text me the address."

Comanche left without saying goodbye and went to an address not exactly on Alton, but on a parallel road, West Avenue. Pérez and Barboza were waiting in an unmarked car with dark tints parked on the corner by the white Hyundai, under the shade of a mango tree. Sergio Barboza had already cased the house, there was only the front door so they'd both go in that way.

"No use of excessive force," said Pérez, "we know who we're dealing with. And keep it down, we grab him, take him home like nothing ever happened here, okay?

COMANCHE, PI | **PEDRO MEDINA LEÓN**

"Alright, Officer Pérez," said Barboza, and Comanche just then took notice of him: lanky, more with the bearing of a judge or Salvadoran bureaucrat than a cop, and the face of a Doberman.

Comanche and Barboza approached the door. Barboza knocked. A pale kid with buggy eyes who looked to be about Mario's age answered. Comanche asked him to please grab Mario Robalca for him. Sensing that the kid had no idea what he meant, Comanche pushed him aside. Inside, bare walls and the silence of empty rooms. The rest of the kids were sitting on the floor eating Pollo Tropical on Styrofoam plates.

"Mario?" asked Comanche.

The kids looked at each other, then him. Comanche was directly in front of them and Barboza had the door blocked.

"Where the fuck is Mario?" Comanche asked.

The buggy eyed kid who'd opened the door was still standing next to Barboza. He spoke up, said they'd be leaving in a minute, that they'd only gone to that house because they knew it was empty and they needed a space to rehearse the play they were putting on at the South Beach Festival of Independent Theater. They had nowhere else to do it.

"Mario Robalca," Comanche said, "we are looking for Mario Robalca, is he with you?"

"Who's that?" they asked.

Comanche showed them Robalca's photo. None of them had ever seen him but just the same, they'd be leaving the house and never coming back.

"Stay as long as you want," said Comanche, slamming the door shut on his way out.

"Sorry, man," said Barboza. "I thought the skinny one sucking on the chicken leg was Mario Robalca. The photo Pérez gave me wasn't very clear, still though, no excuse."

"You're a fucking asshole, Barboza," said Comanche, quieting him. "You're a fucking asshole and I don't have time to waste with fucking assholes."

"Hey, easy man, easy."

"Easy what, asshole," said Comanche getting in Barboza's face, locking eyes with the Salvadorean's Doberman eyes. "You want me to tell Pérez that in addition to wasting my fucking time here, your work over at the Knockout Gym wasn't worth shit either?"

"What are you talking about?"

"I don't have time to waste on fucking assholes, I already told you that. Go tell Pérez how you fucked this up. I'm outta here."

Comanche headed to El Bikini, Skinny would still be there and he'd be able to get ice and limes. He needed a hot shower and a couple of fiestas.

14.

Pérez had a cortadito, and Comanche had a cortadito and a Marlboro. They didn't talk about Barboza's screw-up and Comanche preferred it like that. Then they left Los Latinos in the same unmarked car that Pérez and Barboza had been in the day before. They parked around the corner of Magic City Cars, Battiri's body shop, a warehouse filled with tires, headlights, and bumpers stacked floor-to-ceiling against the walls, the skeletons of a Mustang, a Camaro, and Corvette from the 1960's in various stages of refurbishment.

"How can I help you?" A mechanic in greasy grey overalls asked Comanche.

"Franko Battiri?"

"Who is asking?"

"He wouldn't know but I wanna talk to him," replied Comanche.

Comanche got distracted with the Mustang and when he turned, a longhaired fat guy wearing a Homer Simpson t-shirt that barely covered his large belly.

"Who are you?" asked the fat guy.

"I'm looking for Franko Battiri."

"That's me, what do you want?"

"Mario Robalca," said Comanche, showing the photo.

"Okay, who's that?"

"Tell me where I can find Mario Robalca," said Comanche now showing the photo of Battiri with Mario at Maurice Gibb Park. "You were at his house last Wednesday afternoon and you two argued."

"Who the fuck are you?" said Battiri, shoving Comanche and prompting the rest of the mechanics to form a circle around them.

Comanche's reaction was immediate, pulling the Glock from behind his Levi's, releasing the safety and aiming it at Battiri.

"Maybe we can be clearer with each other, ah, Battiri?"

"Whoah, whoah, relax," said Battiri. "Put that thing down dumbass or this will end poorly for you."

"Tell these fuckers to beat it," said Comanche motioning toward the mechanics. "And we'll talk."

"Who the fuck are you?"

"Ten minutes Battiri, without your entourage."

"Guys," Battiri said, brushing his long hair away, "take a ten-minute break, go!"

Comanche holstered the Glock behind his Levi's and told Battiri that he knew about his loansharking and extorsion racket. Serious crimes he'd be willing to overlook if he told him everything he knew about Mario Robalca who'd been missing since Thursday. Reminding him that he had proof of their meeting on Wednesday.

"You're a fucking cop!"

"No, I'm not, but I'm connected enough to get you hemmed up if you don't start talking."

"Suck my dick."

"I'm offering to keep the cops at bay, Battiri," Comanche repeated. If he didn't talk with Comanche, he'd talk with a pair of uniforms, the difference being that with Comanche his dirty dealings would go unnoticed.

"Fucker, it's not the first time they try to rope me. They don't got shit on me."

"If they do or don't, we'll see," said Comanche. "But if you want to avoid wasting all that time, this is your last chance. Start talking."

"Oh, poor kid," said Battiri in a mocking tone. "Is his daddy looking for him? Is Marito lost? Fucking cop faggot."

Comanche took out his cigarettes, offering him one.

"Okay Battiri, keep talking, so far you haven't said shit, and my patience is running out. In less than five minutes I can get three units outside and have this place shut down while they drag your ass down to the station."

"Mario Robalca…" started Battiri, immediately clarifying he'd only talk to get Comanche out of his shop, had been his client for years. Sucked at repaying his debts but was quick, agile and punched hard. One time he'd left his dad's Cartier as collateral and Battiri had pawned it since he never recouped his cash on the loan. Mario challenged him to a fight at the body shop afterhours. Battiri had figured it would be a piece of cake, given the obvious size and weight difference but Marito, who'd shown up in a Muhammad Ali tee and boxing gloves, made quick work of him with three quick righthanded jabs to the face and a brutal left uppercut on his way down that had one of his eyes swollen shut for over a week. Battiri's guys had to jump in and grab Robalca. Even after getting his ass whupped, Battiri kept lending him money since the kid always had valuable collateral. The last thing he'd left was a set of high-end silverware, last

Wednesday, that he still had in his office. That's why he'd been by, he had lent him two grand.

"Why did you argue?"

"Because that fucker wanted more money."

"What did Mario need the money for?"

"What for?"

"Yeah, what for?"

"Drugs? Bitches? Booze? What else a young man on South Beach need money for?"

"Where do you think he is?"

Battiri didn't know and he could care less. But it would be in Mario Robalca's best interest to show up and pay up or the silverware was getting pawned next week – even if *Marito* came at him angry and ready to box.

"How often did he borrow from you?"

"At least once a month."

"Always that much?"

"No way, it was never more than $300 or so."

"Okay," said Comanche. "Call your dog's back in. I'm outta here."

Comanche walked up to the squad car and told Pérez he could go; it had been a good idea to come to Battiri's but now he had more questions than answers. He'd have to keep looking but he'd call him later if he had any news. Pérez asked him if he wanted a ride anywhere and Comanche told him it wouldn't be necessary. As the squad car rounded the corner, Comanche pulled out his phone and Marlboros.

"Hey, bro," answered Consorte.

"I need to talk with Papito," said Comanche.

"When?"

"Now, let me get his number."

"No bro, can't do that, but I can call him for you right now. Gimmie a minute."

Comanche sat on a white block on the corner that had the street name written on it and took a long drag on his Marlboro. If Mario Robalca needed that much cash and wasn't gambling, it had to be some other vice and Papito was the king of vices on Miami Beach. He didn't finish his smoke when he got a text from Consorte: Papito would be at Ilusiones in thirty minutes.

15.

"I think you can help me out," said Comanche, looking at Papito from head to toe. He was wearing baggy purple pants, air-pumped Nike's, Prada glasses, and a black shirt printed with a rapper's face smoking a blunt.

"Whatever you need, boss."

"*Cocaconlichis* to quench your thirsts," said Consorte dropping off a bottle of Coca-Cola and pair of glasses at the table. "If you need anything else, I'm behind the bar."

"Thanks, brother," said Papito.

Gitano and Runcho behind bars was a vengeance Papito had dreamed of to honor Nené's memory. He had his boys on the inside keeping watch and every week, Gitano and

Runcho received a friendly reminder of who they'd fucked with. They'd left Gitano blind in one eye already, stomping his head until he lost consciousness. His eye popped out like a jellied marble. He'd ordered them to slice up Runcho's ear and Maraca, the biggest black guy on the block, raped him. But this one backfired since Runcho sought out Maraca afterwards for another round.

"You know this guy?" asked Comanche, placing Mario Robalca's photo next to the Coca-Cola bottle.

"Lemme see," said Papito, grabbing the photo and holding it close to his eye. "No boss, don't know him."

"Shit," said Comanche, slamming his fist on the table.

"Who is he?"

"Mario Robalca."

"What's up with him?"

"Missing since last week," said Comanche, "with two grand from a loan shark that he put as collateral his parent's silverware."

Comanche thought the money might be for drugs.

"Wait, two grand you said?"

"Yeah, two grand."

"That's a serious wad, you ever heard of the Delirio raves?"

Delirio were popup raves that went down on the beach, by the water, at night. Locations changed constantly to keep the cops at bay. Lots of drugs, lots of booze. With that kind of cash, one could go on a serious bender for days.

"There was a Delirio rave last Friday, we handle supply, know what I mean?"

"Where?"

"Hey bro, let me get another one," Papito said, holding up the empty cola bottle, letting out a loud burp to get Consorte's attention. He couldn't remember exactly where it happened but one of his guys had been there to move merch.

"Put me in touch," said Comanche.

"Gotcha boss, Mario Robalca, right?"

"Yes."

"Let me take a picture of that photo with my cell."

"How do we go about this?"

"Gimmie your number and I'll call you but answer, it's gonna be from a private number."

"Okay."

They shook hands and Comanche excused himself.

"Hello, Pérez?"

"Yes, Comanche."

16.

The special of the day at Los Latinos was plantain soup and pork rinds. Comanche ordered the rinds with rice and sweet fried plantains and a Coca-Cola, Officer Pérez the same but with rice and yucca in *mojo criollo* and an iced tea.

"Barboza told me you had words with him," started Pérez.

"He's incompetent."

"Why do you say that?"

"Because he is."

"The Heat are playing for their lives tonight," said Pérez, hoping to change the topic.

"Didn't know that."

"How can you not know?"

"To be honest, I don't give a fuck."

The previous night, as Officer Pérez closed for the night and was about leave his office, he got a call from Major Tito Robalca. The Major waited outside, dressed in sweats since he'd been out for his usual walk down the Venetian Causeway. He immediately asked Pérez about his son and if he had any news from Comanche. Although that was just a way to vent. His son was neck-deep in drugs, and he had known it for a long time, feeling responsible. He was never there for Mario, not even when he was a child. Never played catch in the park or taught him how to ride a bike. It was always Lidia who took charge; he, in his patrol car chasing prostitutes and dealers on the corners of Washington Avenue, let the years of his son's upbringing slip by. And as Mario grew into adolescence, Major Tito Robalca also grew professionally, and although he was no longer behind the wheel of a patrol car, he oversaw an entire unit, seated at his desk, and that was very demanding. He would come home when Lidia and Mario were already asleep, and if he managed to leave at a decent time and they waited for him with dinner on the table, the main course would be shouting at Lidia. His marriage had sunk. Sometimes Mario would intervene, raising his voice in defense of his mother, and in return, he'd get a slap in the face or a punch that confined him to his room for three or four days, waiting for the bruises or swelling to subside. All the crap that was happening was his fault, Major Tito Robalca kept repeating. Absolutely all of it. The only thing he wanted was for Comanche to find Mario so he could be admitted to a rehab center and try to salvage their relationship. He would also leave the house; he and Lidia were old, and he should've done it long ago, but out of cowardice, out of fear of a lonely old age, he hadn't dared. His hand never shook when he had to exchange fire in the alleys of Miami Beach, but he pissed his pants at the thought of silence in his house after his work routine. It was better to have someone to fight with, someone to yell at, with the voices of Univision reporters as background noise and the microwave's beep accentuating the aroma of freshly nuked lentils.

"Rice and yucca?" asked the waiter, holding a tray with their food.

"Here," said Pérez, motioning to the placemat in front of him.

"Hmm, these are good," said Comanche, savoring the first bite of pork rinds.

"Really good, I told you," replied Pérez.

"You ever eat at La Carreta?"

"It's been years, I hardly leave the Beach these days."

"You should go back, you'd love it."

"I'll ask Romero, maybe the three of us can meet up one day," said Pérez, "you ever try his wife Nancy's cooking?"

"No."

"It's hands down, the best Cuban food I've ever tried."

"You've spoken to Romero these days?"

"Oh yeah, earlier actually. He wanted to know how things were going. He complained that you don't answer his calls."

"Nah, he thinks I'm gonna talk more with him than my girl," said Comanche.

"He's always been like that. Pass the salt?"

"Does Romero know Robalca?"

"Just by name. Robalca was first with the North Miami Beach PD and Romero had just retired when he transferred to South Beach."

"So Robalca came clean," said Comanche switching gears, handing Pérez a small caddie with the salt and pepper shakers.

"Didn't see that coming," said Pérez. Major Tito Robalca was a man of few words, serious, stoic. A 'hard man' if he had to describe him. They'd worked together for years and used to go out for beers on Friday nights at Joe's on the Venetian. Their conversations were always about sports or work, never anything personal.

"His guilty conscience finally won," Comanche said. "From day one you could tell he wasn't telling us everything about his kid."

"It's a shame."

"Wait a minute," Comanche said, waving a finger at Pérez to be silent, his phone was vibrating, it was a blocked number.

"Boss," said Papito on the line.

"What's up?"

"You know El Chuzo?"

"The Colombian joint on 5th Street and Washington?"

"Yeah."

"Okay."

"La Bichota will be waiting for you there tomorrow, bright and early."

"Who the fuck's La Bichota?"

"La Bichota," said Papito, "was our buyer for that rave Friday. She was with the guy in the photo you showed me at Ilusiones, my boy recognized him."

"She can't see me now?"

"No boss, she's in Orlando but she gets back tonight."

Comanche put his phone away and took another bite of the pork.

"Good news?" asked Pérez.

"It's the contact for a friend of Mario's, she's probably the last one who saw him. She's meeting me tomorrow."

"She can't today?"

"Nope, she's in Orlando."

"Shit."

Comanche changed the subject and asked, out of curiosity, what had become of La Casa de Muñecas, he'd been by but didn't see the sign. Luciano Piccini was in processing, he was looking at 10 to 13 years of jailtime, and the waiter the same for being an accomplice. The problem was that the whores had now moved outside to the corner of Española and Washington Avenue. The cops were on it, but every time they picked one up, two took their place. The corner was hot, too many whores, too many drugs.

The waitress, wearing a black t-shirt emblazoned with the 'Here, we're all proud Cholos!' slogan came by the table and asked them if they wanted anything else. Comanche ordered a cortadito and Pérez a *café con leche* and the bill.

17.

Comanche took his shirt off, lit a Marlboro, and opened the Bacardí rum that patiently waited on the nightstand.

"Babe, where have you been?" asked Mariolys on the phone. She had called him a few times after her shift at El Dolarazo in the Mall of the Americas.

"Busy day."

"Do you know when you'll be back?"

"No, not yet."

"I wanna show you the apartment," said Mariolys who'd been out with Luz buying sheets, cups and utensils at Walmart. "And I want to celebrate!"

Comanche agreed with her, squeezing half a lime into his glass.

Miami was starting to make sense for Mariolys. Years ago, when her high school classmates talked about their college plans at Florida International University or in other states, she didn't say anything: she had just arrived from Camagüey with her mom and dad. Their rush was for the girl to finish school and start working to help with household expenses and get ahead in the big city. The little money her dad made as a security guard at a furniture store and her mom as a grocery bagger at Varadero Supermarket wasn't enough to start a new life. They had agreed on that in Cuba, when they sat in the living room making plans to leave and gossiping over a Sears seasonal catalog her mom had managed to get. Seeing that catalog made them even more eager to leave the island. In those pages were things they didn't even know existed, things completely unknown in Cuba, like a box that looked like it was brought from Mars, used in the kitchen where you'd put dirty dishes in and they'd came out spotless.

As soon as Mariolys graduated from high school, she

got a job as a cashier at Las Lilas Flower Shop, Monday to Friday, and another one on the weekends bagging groceries at Winn-Dixie. She liked her job at Las Lilas; the flowers, with their colors and smells, made her happy. Las Lilas was close to her house, in the heart of Little Havana overlooking the Domino Park, just five minutes away by bike, but she would leave a little earlier to stop by the small coffee window half a block from the flower shop, to buy a cortadito and ham croquetas and have breakfast at work. She earned her little bit of money and was content; Thursday was her day off, which coincided with her mom's. And what a feast they would have at Versailles: ropa vieja, picadillo, *congrí*, *arroz imperial*. Whatever they wanted, without checking the prices. Then they'd go to Sears on Coral Way. Emotionally, though, nothing much transpired in her love life in Miami. She had a couple of encounters with guys. One her cousin Luz introduced her to from church, a real Jesus freak, the guy would stay on Sundays praying and helping the pastor, but when they went out dancing at Las Tabernas de Wancho, after half an hour he tried to grope Mariolys and suggested going to a motel and splitting the bill.

The other was an Ecuadorian businessman she met on a Friday night while dancing at Ball and Chain. They ended the night in a glass tower on Brickell Avenue, with a uniformed concierge and marble floors. The apartment belonged to the company, at the top of the tower. They went up in an elevator with a digital button panel that felt like a spaceship taking off. They got comfortable on a white leather couch. He folded his jacket, placed it on the back, poured himself two fingers of Glenlivet with an ice cube. He offered her a glass of Rioja or Chardonnay. She asked for beer. An ice-cold Presidente. The Ecuadorian businessman only had Corona cans in the minibar. From the couch, they saw other glass towers scratching the sky, a few apartment lights shining like a ring of fireflies, yachts that looked insignificant in the blackness of the night. He was returning to Ecuador on Sunday. His wife and children were waiting for him. She didn't care about his commitment. With that view, she felt like JLo. This is how JLo must screw, from the sky, equal to the stars, above everything and everyone. She downed the remaining Corona in one gulp, left the can on the floor, took off her light brown linen blouse, the one she only wore when she went dancing at Ball and Chain, and her bra, and climbed on top of the Ecuadorian.

"Either tomorrow or the day after I'll have that figured out."

Comanche was about to fix himself his third and final fiesta since he had to be on point the following morning, but he thought it would be best to enjoy it at the Al Capone since it was early and there was no Heat game on. That way he wouldn't be stuck between four walls for too long. Outside, he lit up a cigarette and walked down 13th Street towards Meridian, the shady avenue that was flanked on both sides by enormous trees and looked like a forest. He fantasized lately about locking himself away in one of those second-floor efficiencies, with a balcony and views of Flamingo Park, to make himself a fiesta and smoke a cigarette, rather than at that one-bedroom apartment waiting for him on Flagler Avenue with white sheets from Walmart.

Wild Cat, Lasticön, La Chica más pop de South Beach, Cabalito, Peru and his girlfriend, la Cololo, were doing Jäger shots at the bar, and every time Karina bent down to grab a glass, she'd take a shot too from a bottle she had hidden under the bar.

"Rum," asked Comanche.

"He's here! The boss of all bosses!" said Karina, disinhibited by the Jägermeister.

"Welcome, copper," said Cabalito, toasting his glass towards him.

Comanche shook hands with everyone in the group and sat on a stool.

"How's the case going?" asked Karina, putting Comanche's drink on the bar on top of the caricatured Al Capone coaster.

"Good, good so far."

"Staying longer on the Beach, or will you be leaving soon?"

"No clue yet."

Wild Cat went through La Chica más pop de South Beach, Peru and La Cololo and stood beside Comanche at the bar, patting him on the shoulder as he ordered a glass of water. He was done with the Jägers since he had an early morning the following day doing research at the public library. From 8 a.m. until noon at the library and from 2 to 7 p.m. writing in his efficiency on Drexel Avenue, that was his routine.

"Whatchu writing about this time?" asked Comanche.

"About the Mutiny," replied Wild Cat. "It was a boutique hotel in Coconut Grove that gained notoriety during the '80s for its wild ass parties. It was *the* hotel to stay at in the U.S., shit, maybe even the whole world. Politicians, artists, the rich and famous, you name it, but the most interesting fixtures there were all the high-level caporegimes who partied there. Cocaine Cowboys too, and that opened the door to the Colombian cartels, Pablo Escobar, Griselda."

"Hmm, interesting."

"That's right," said Wild Cat, "this city is full of treasures like that, only problem is this city also doesn't know how to preserve its history."

"I read your piece on the Bee Gees; I had no clue about that."

"See what I mean?"

Wild Cat couldn't understand why Miami's tourism appeal was hopping on some bullshit ferry at Bayside to go gawk at the mansions of Fisher Island where the Estefans and Lionel Richie lived.

"You know anything of Muhammad Ali's time in Miami?" asked Comanche. The Robalca business, his fixation on the sport, and his idolizing of Ali had spurred a little curiosity.

"Of course, during segregation in the '60s, Ali was in Miami all the time. He trained here. The Beatles even visited him at the gym he trained at."

"Know that gym's address?"

"Well, not exactly," said Wild Cat, adding that the spot still stood but was abandoned. The city had never gotten it together to protect it by registering it with the National Register of Historic Places. It had even operated as a different boxing gym until a few years ago."

Wild Cat finished his glass of water and was about to leave. He still owed Comanche the chat and the article about boxing, but if he kept talking about Miami, he'd get excited and order another drink—the subject was too long and way too interesting to him. Comanche said they'd leave together; he had that meeting with La Bichota the next morning. One more drink, and he'd end up going to the dude who sold him coke before in the bar's bathroom, exchanging a rolled-up bill slipped to him near the sink, in a basket where the guy sold Halls candies and Juicy Fruit mint gum. At the door, they parted ways since they were going in opposite directions. A bit further, at the corner of Española and Washington

Avenue, Comanche saw the blue and red flashing lights of a squad car reflecting on the windows of the Black Ink Tattoo Shop. A policeman was shining his flashlight onto a woman's golden hair, her red lips, her generous cleavage, and her legs wrapped in black leather up to her knees. The woman was handcuffed, her jaw pressed against the trunk, with her small black purse on the pavement. She searched for it with her foot, and on the asphalt rolled a lipstick, a small bottle of sweet-smelling perfume, mouthwash, eyebrow liner, nail polish, face powder, and condoms.

18.

Comanche didn't need to hide his eyes from South Beach's brutal sun behind his Ray-Ban aviators since the sky was a swollen gray canopy that could pop at any moment and piss all over the streets. El Chuzo was completely drowned in the thick smell of condiments and pork rinds, and the walls were covered with photos of James Rodríguez, René Higuita, Radamel Falcao, el Pibe Valderrama, and Colombian flags. A pair of speakers on the green Formica bar were blasting Bomba Estéreo:

Dice que Colombia es combate, ambiente
Sonidos y ritmos listos pa la gente

Listo que te vamo' a poner a gozá'

Listo que te vamo' a pone' a vacilá'

"Bichota?" asked Comanche.

The woman behind the register had an angular face, sharp like an axe, mahogany colored. She was dressed in black, green bangs falling over her forehead, and her head was shaved on the sides. She wore a nose ring, her eyes were metallic blue, and her fingernails were chewed up.

"Mapache?"

"Comanche."

"Yeah, well, sorry."

"Where is Mario Robalca?" asked Comanche, not interested in pussyfooting.

"Something to drink, coffee maybe?"

"I need to find Mario."

"Whoa, look at this guy!" said La Bichota, "I'm just trying to be polite here."

"Yes, thank you for the coffee. I need your help finding Mario Robalca," said Comanche as he sat down on one of the barstools.

Mario Robalca and La Bichota met at Miami Beach Senior High School. Mario went on to study Business at Miami Dade College, but he wasn't interested—he only wanted to keep his dad from hassling him about sleeping until noon. The only thing he ever felt a passion for was boxing, but his dad never wanted to support him in that 'sport of blacks and mobsters.' After high school, Mario and La Bichota went separate ways, she was planning to study graphic design, though she didn't yet know when or where. For now, she was living in an efficiency with her dad and wasn't sure if she wanted to stay in Miami or move to Atlanta or Gainesville. They still saw each other, sometimes at the beach, sometimes at a bar. It was leaving one of those bars on Española Way that he told her he wasn't going home to sleep. He had a huge argument with his dad. When Mario was a kid and later as a teenager, if he brought home bad grades, his dad would drag him into the shower under cold water, make him take off his shirt, and whip his back with an electrical cord. The same happened whenever he did something that Major Tito Robalca didn't like. But Mario didn't take it anymore, he defended himself, and that night, they came to blows. Mario dodged one punch after another, and when he was about to throw a right hook at his dad's exposed face, the presence of his mom stopped him.

They left behind the bar on Española. Mario rummaged through his pockets. In his left pocket, he had a little baggie of coke, which he showed to La Bichota. In the other pocket, he had a thick wad of cash, he'd pawned some of his dad's silver medals, one of his prized police decorations. That coke would be his companion for the rest of the night. La Bichota asked if he wanted company, and Mario said yes. Taking turns going to the bathroom, they drained pitchers of Pabst Blue Ribbon at Lost Saturday until the bar lights came on, "The Passenger" by Iggy Pop started playing, and when it ended, Jhonny Love, the DJ, turned off the music and approached them. The three of them headed to the Deuce bar but didn't go in—something happened at the door, though La Bichota never understood what. She was looking at the ground, at the frayed hem of her black jeans being torn apart by the heel of her black Vans, and Jhonny Love was peeing on the tire of a convertible Mazda Miata parked in the alleyway.

Maybe it was just Mario's madness, but he got into a whirlwind of fists with the security guard at the door, a huge King Kong of a guy. And yet, King Kong collapsed onto the sidewalk. Mario's lip was the only thing bleeding, which La Bichota wiped clean with her checkered flannel shirt, and at the Art Deco Supermarket, they bought some band-aids and a bottle of Grant's that Mario uncapped and took a sip from to relax. The cashier told them that was prohibited and threatened to call the cops. Mario let out a loud burp, and Love, who knew the cashier, calmed down the situation. They left. Washington Avenue was a parade of uniforms and flashing blue and red lights hunting for dealers, hookers, gunmen, and crazies like the three of them. Mario hid the bottle inside his pants, and they walked toward the beach on Ocean Drive. The sand was swarming with couples screwing, moaning with pleasure. They climbed up into a lifeguard tower, where a homeless man was masturbating to the low-budget porn playing out in front of him, undisturbed by their presence. La Bichota took off her black Vans, the hem of her jeans damp from stepping through puddles and piss. Jhonny Love started crying. He always cried when he got high. He remembered his childhood and teenage years in Edinburgh, where he lived with his grandmother until he was 13, then survived on the streets stealing cars. His mother was a heroin addict and a bar waitress, and she never knew the face of the man who had lifted her skirt from behind to fuck her in the bar's bathroom. When Jhonny was eighteen, he and his gang of thieves pulled off a big heist, stealing a Lamborghini with a briefcase inside that had 20 thousand pounds. They split it in fours, and with his share, he bought a ticket to New York, where he worked for 3 years, during the day at a McDonald's drive-thru and at night drying glasses at a bar until he slowly worked his way behind the DJ booth. He'd always wanted to be a DJ at a punk bar, ever since his years in Edinburgh when Joe Strummer, Morrissey, and Sid Vicious were the soundtrack. Later, he moved to Atlanta and, after time, ended up in Miami.

La Bichota was the least complicated of the group. She liked a little coke, acid, and mushrooms here and there, but it was just for fun—she could go weeks without using anything.

That's how the Delirio raves began. At first, it was the three of them wandering down Washington Avenue, under the amber glow of the cascades of light falling from the streetlamps, with glazed eyes lost in the labyrinth of neon pizza shops and tattoo parlors. Mario Robalca with a bottle of Grant's tucked inside his pants, coke, and cash in his pockets, La Bichota dragging her jeans and biting her nails, and Johnny Love feeling like a punk lost among the palm trees of South Beach. They would take refuge in an alleyway and snort coke. It climbed up their insides like a speeding elevator crashing into their brains.

Their hearts racing, by 4 or 5 in the morning, they would find refuge in a lifeguard station. Gradually, acquaintances from the long, rough nights in South Beach joined them, and the pilgrimage down Washington turned into a gathering on the beach. Each one arrived with bottles of tequila, vodka, whiskey, and all sorts of drugs.

"As you can see, I'm in the same boat as you."

"Why?" asked Comanche.

"Help yourself," said La Bichota, placing the steaming cup of coffee on the bar.

La Bichota had called Mario several times, and he hadn't answered. After the last Delirio rave, La Bichota wanted a detox and told Mario and Johnny to go to Orlando for the weekend to indulge in roller coasters, hamburgers, hot dogs, French fries, and ice cream with Mickey Mouse ears. They agreed to talk on Saturday, but he never replied again. La Bichota wanted to take Mario with her because she'd seen him in bad shape, and not just because of drugs, but because of the last fight he had with his dad. La Bichota didn't ask why they had fought, and he didn't tell her either; in fact, Mario, who was wearing a Muhammad Ali t-shirt, barely spoke to her, he was anxious and didn't even wait to reach the beach: taking a full bump of coke right in public.

"And Jhonny Love? You saw him over the weekend?"

"He came with me, and he tried calling Mario too but nothing."

"Where do you think he's holing up?"

"His escape was drugs," she said, "but then he'd get all guilty about it the next day, and he'd lock himself up to box to work the shit out of his system. The guilt always won, and he'd swear each time was the last time and that he'd go all in with the boxing to stay clean."

"Where did he box? He wasn't doing that at home."

"No, and definitely not at any of these newer gyms that are all over the Beach. He had his own VIP spot, according to him anyways."

"Do you know where?"

"No sir, I don't."

"Okay," said Comanche, taking a few moments to organize his thoughts. "Hmm, maybe I do... yeah." He got up, pushing the stool up against the bar.

"You gonna finish your coffee?"

He didn't reply. He walked out of El Chuzo. In the background, growing fainter as he walked away, continued Bomba Estéreo:

¡Y grita fuego!
Mantenlo prendido ¡fueeego!
No lo dejes apagar

Y no lo dejes apagá
Y no lo dejes apagá
Y no lo dejes apagá

19.

"Sir," said Wild Cat on the line.

"Brother, I need the address to the gym where Muhammad Ali trained."

"Yeah, gimmie a sec, let me look for it."

"Text me when you have it, it's urgent."

"Yessir."

"Thanks," said Comanche, putting his aviators on even though the sky was even grayer than before.

Wild Cat's directions led Comanche to the first blocks of Alton Road, at the corner of 5th Street. He had been there before, but from the outside, it was impossible to recognize that this place, which at first glance looked like a closed laundromat, was Ali's gym. The front door was sealed with a rusty padlock; Comanche circled the building, and the back door opened with just a turn of the handle. He was greeted by narrow stairs. On the second floor, the first thing he saw was a torn couch with no cushions, a burnt bare bulb in the ceiling, and on the walls, faded black and white posters of Muhammad Ali, Angelo Dundee, and Mantequilla Nápoles. After that, the larger space, the main room, was lit only by the rays of sunlight filtering through small windows. In that place, the smells of closed doors, rough nights, sweat, and decaying bodies mingled. The walls were also covered with posters of boxers, the most eye-catching being the one of Muhammad Ali with the Beatles in a boxing session in that same space years earlier. And in the center, the ring, surrounded by broken or frayed blue ropes.

As Comanche walked through the room, the smell grew more uncomfortable and penetrating, coming from the corner where the punching bags were. There were many, a forest of bags. It was an unmistakable odor, a penetrating stench that made him gag, and he covered his nose with the sleeve of his shirt. He dodged one bag. Then another, and another. At the end of the forest hung the body of Mario Robalca from a chain. His pupils were dilated, two black holes staring into the void, and dried vomit on his chest over Muhammad Ali's face on the shirt. His skin was greenish. His face was swollen.

Without taking his sleeve off his nose, Comanche walked out. The posters. The ring. The stairs. Outside, he chucked up a yellowish mixture of food, bile, and rum on a discarded Burger King wax wrapper. He burped, the taste of his vomit permeating his palate again. He put his hand in his pocket and took out his Marlboros and phone. As he called Officer Pérez, the clouds finally burst, pissing all over the sidewalks and palm trees of South Beach.

20.

"Two for twenty," said Comanche, putting a pair of bills into the center pocket.

"*Marico*, you're gonna leave me broke as fuck," exclaimed Chamizo who already knew Comanche would beat his ass and take his cash, but regardless, he still took the bet, thinking of it as an investment in bettering his skills.

"Is there a problem?" asked Comanche as he put a cigarette in his mouth.

There wasn't a problem, not really, but Chamizo was going to get together with some friends later to watch the

Heat game, and he needed his cash to pick up a six-pack…
but he'd take the bet anyway.

"Here are the croquetas and sodas, my friends," said
Consorte. "Who's paying for this?"

"The loser," said Comanche as he racked the balls in the
triangle.

"Fuck," said Chamizo under his breath.

Back at the bar, Consorte put on Héctor Lavoe's "El
Cantante," winking to Comanche that it was dedicated to
him by singing along and changing the lyrics:

> *Yo, soy el Comanche*
> *Que hoy han venido a escuchar*
> *Lo mejor del repertorio*
> *A ustedes voy a brindar*

"You ever find the guy you were looking for?" asked
Chamizo.

"Yes, I did," said Comanche, the image of Mario Robalca's limp body and empty, black eyes still fresh in his mind.

"Ah, cool, thank god."

"Wanna break?" asked Comanche.

"Sure."

Chamizo struck the white ball, which was a clean hit with lots of power, and the balls dispersed all over the green felt.

"You're solids," said Comanche, pointing out that the blue ball had gone into the corner pocket.

"Where are you going to watch the Heat game?" asked Chamizo as he examined the angles for banking the yellow ball.

Comanche wasn't interested in that. Even though Karina – who'd forgotten that he'd passed by the bar when she was drunk on Jägermeister – had texted him asking if everything was okay since he'd left her place that day to answer the phone. She invited him to the Al Capone since the whole gang would be there to watch the game. He preferred the bit of Bacardí he had left at El Bikini, just the booze, no cocaine since he had to be up early the next day to head back home to Little Havana. Romero had a new case waiting for him.

"Ball in hand, you tapped the white ball," said Comanche. "My turn."

"*Coño 'e la madre,*" exclaimed Chamizo.

"Put the volume up," asked Comanche, turning his back to the bar to set up his shot.

Y sigo mi vida
Con risas y penas
Con ratos amargos
Y con cosas buenas

MONTHS LATER

Fucking Fridays.

Romero dismissed him from the new case. It was some sculptor who kept getting his shit stolen out of his Little Havana studio. Comanche thought something was off with his story, dates and times weren't gelling. He felt he was wasting his time. He pressed on. The sculptor raised his voice, "What more do you want me to say, eh?" Comanche didn't like that, pushed him, and the sculptor fell backward into a corner full of paint cans, hitting his ribs, and staining his white shirt with red and yellow paint.

"I don't want to see you around here; please do me the favor of leaving," said Romero in his office, not taking his eyes off him until Comanche crossed the door's threshold. He headed to the Aruba to lower the decibels of anger bursting in his mind by drowning them in the rums his buddy, Tony el Vasco, would pour.

One.

Two.

Three.

And he left with a little platinum packet of cocaine for later. His next stop was at the Varadero Supermarket, where he bought soy sauce, green onions, eggs, rice, chicken thighs, lemons, and sesame oil. He was going to make fried rice. At Licores Catrachos he got a bottle of Bacardí. Then he headed to the one-bedroom apartment on Flagler Avenue, where he climbed the three flights of stairs; the elevator was broken, and there were no signs that it would be repaired any time soon. He would wait for Mariolys with food and fiestas; she got off work from El Dolarazo at six. Before entering the apartment, he checked the mailbox; Mariolys was expecting a little check from the government. Among the accumulated paperwork from several days, he found discount coupons from Sedano's, bankruptcy lawyer ads, the latest offers on T-Mobile plans, and a large envelope addressed to him. No government check. He left the Varadero bag on the kitchen counter, unbuttoned his Levi's, and took off his shirt. Inside the envelope was a handwritten note that said: "Inspector, you're going to like this. Hopefully, we'll see you around here soon. Wild Cat." It was the latest issue of *Revólver*, dedicated to the history of boxing in South Beach. The Comanche prepared a fiesta with a splash of Coca-Cola, plenty of ice and lime, sprawled out on the couch, and set aside *Ciudad Maldita*, Lizárraga's novel that had gone largely unnoticed on his nightstand since he returned from his last case in South Beach. But Mariolys, despite not being a reader, had opened it a couple of nights ago when insomnia got the better of her and devoured it because she identified with the colorful characters from Miami.

By Wild Cat

The Southern Star

The first memorial erected for an African American man on Miami Beach was for Cassius Clay at the Miami Beach Convention Center.

The sunrises of Miami Beach were disrupted in 1961 when an African American man began running along the MacArthur Causeway every day at five in the morning. The man was very tall and robust, a perfect silhouette. Racial segregation was so brutal at that time that a person of color couldn't walk down the street if the sky was dark. The Civil

Rights Act, which sought to end that situation, wasn't signed until 1964.

The first time Cassius Clay (Louisville, Kentucky, 1942 – Scottsdale, Arizona, 2016) stepped into a boxing ring, he was 12 years old, and from that moment, he knew he wanted to be a world champion. That became his priority, more than school. Success came early: at 18, he won a gold medal at the 1960 Rome Olympics. To solidify his career, he needed a sponsor, but boxing was not a bona fide sport for Black athletes, and the only ones backing Black boxers were mobsters, and working for the mafia wasn't an option. He had to knock on many doors until The Louisville Group gave him their support.

Clay's training began in San Diego, but it didn't prosper due to a lack of understanding with his coach. Then, the opportunity arose to move south, to Miami, to train with Angelo Dundee, whom he fortunately knew. Cassius Clay landed at Miami International Airport at the age of 21 with the firm conviction to dethrone the champion, Sonny Liston.

He settled in a motel on Biscayne Boulevard and immediately started his routine: he would get up at five in the morning, train by jogging along the MacArthur Causeway to the 5th Street Gym on Washington Avenue—the place where he had a historic meeting with The Beatles during their trip to perform on The Ed Sullivan Show at the Deauville Hotel in Miami Beach, which catapulted them to fame. Clay would spend hours in the gym, avoiding any excesses with food or drink. As he honed his boxing skills, it was in the South where he converted to Islam to openly fight for equality and defend the rights of his race. Islamic leaders supported him. Malcolm X even traveled to Miami to spend some time with him, which led to his complete ostracization by society.

With 19 fights, all in his favor, Cassius Clay challenged Sonny Liston. The fight was scheduled for February 25 at the Miami Beach Convention Hall. Liston, 12 years older, who had trained in the Missouri State Penitentiary and was sponsored by the mafia, saw the challenge as an audacious move. Insults and threats were exchanged between the two, although the odds were in Liston's favor—he was a great boxer... he was the champion.

Clay's strategy in the fight was to physically exhaust his opponent and knock him out between the seventh and eighth rounds. Sonny Liston, on the other hand, came out to kill. Cassius Clay was battling both Liston and the hostility of nearly nine thousand spectators, except for a few, like Malcolm X, who was sitting very close to his friend's corner. The first three rounds went to Clay, but in the fourth, he began to lose his vision, and Liston gained ground. It's almost proven that during the break between the third and fourth rounds, Liston's corner ordered a poisonous substance to be sprayed on his gloves to blind his opponent. By the end of the fifth round, Clay had recovered, and in the sixth, he attacked so fiercely that Liston asked to stop the fight before coming out for the seventh round. He retired to the hospital with a dislocated shoulder, deep cuts on his face, broken ribs, and two missing teeth. Meanwhile, at the Miami Beach Convention Hall, the new heavyweight champion, euphoric and delirious, shouted at the journalists and the public to swallow their words.

REVÓLVER
EDICIONES

Revólver Ediciones is a publication by undocumented writers and journalists clandestinely operating within Miami Beach.

By Wild Cat

Miami's Knockout

During the 1960s, a second floor in South Beach made Miami the world's boxing mecca.

Miami is a city of many faces. One, very attractive to film and television, is from the 1980s—the paradise of drugs and crime of the Cocaine Cowboys. Another is the resort city, with its coastline lined with the most glamorous five-star towers in the country. There's also the face of Miami as the capital of Cuban exile, when Fidel Castro's dictatorship took control of the island. However, in the hidden corners of Miami, there are more faces, less exposed but no less important, and one of them is that of the boxing mecca, led by the Dundee brothers, Chris and Angelo.

When Chris Dundee first traveled to Miami, the city was a prosperous seaside paradise: World War II had just ended, and the transfer of troops to South Florida, which they used as a base for military training, left a substantial amount of money circulating. Dundee, a boxing promoter and entrepreneur looking to distance himself from the mafia controlling boxing in Nevada, Philadelphia, Los Angeles, and New York, saw potential in Miami and did not hesitate to return.

Chris Dundee began his work by organizing fights on Tuesdays at the Miami Beach Auditorium, attracting the attention of fans, the press, and major boxers. With a defined schedule of fights, the next step for Chris was to create a space where boxers could train and prepare. On a corner of 5th Street and Washington Avenue in South Beach, on an unassuming second floor, he opened the doors of The 5th Street Gym, alongside his brother, the legendary trainer Angelo Dundee. An iconic postcard of Miami is the one where The Beatles are seen with Muhammad Ali during their visit to the gym while he was following his exercise routine. Although Ali's presence brought the world's spotlight to Miami's boxing scene, especially in 1964 with his epic fight against Sonny Liston—a historic bout that drew more than eight hundred journalists—The 5th Street Gym had already positioned itself at the top of a small elite of five gyms, which included Gleason's, Stillman's, and Furkie's in New York, and The Main Street Gym in Los Angeles. No world title contender could avoid training in Miami; in total, 12 titles came out of there, and on its long list of prominent boxers were Roberto "Manos de Piedra" Durán, **Mantequilla** Nápoles, Sonny Liston, Joe Louis, Willie Pastrano, and many others.

If there's one thing Miami struggles to preserve, is its history, which is why it often goes unnoticed. The Bee Gees' recording and rehearsal studio, for example, is now an oil-change workshop. The stage where Jim Morrison and his band, The Doors, played their last show was demolished—a fate that seems to await the legendary Playhouse theater in the Coconut Grove neighborhood. The 5th Street Gym was no exception. The building located at 501 5th Street and Washington Avenue, where it stood for three decades, was demolished, and a parking lot was built in its place, though today a CVS pharmacy operates there. Since then, The 5th Street Gym has changed locations and owners, and while it has lost the prestige that once set it apart, it still holds a special charm for the people of South Beach, including the Scottish author Irvine Welsh, who spends his mornings amidst the forest of hanging punching bags or in the ring.

REVÓLVER
EDICIONES

Revólver Ediciones is a publication by undocumented writers and journalists clandestinely operating within Miami Beach.

About the Author

Pedro Medina León was born in Lima, Peru, in 1977. His novel *Varsovia* won the 2017 Florida Book Award, and he is the author of several books, including *Mañana no te veré en Miami, Marginal, Tour: A Journey Through Miami's Pop Culture, Americana, La chica más pop de South Beach, Callejeros,* and *Bandidos.* He is also the editor of the anthologies *Viaje One Way, Miami (Un) Plugged* and *Noir Tropical.*

About the Translator

Abel M. Folgar is a poet from Caracas, Venezuela of Lebanese and Corsican heritage. He's the author of *Renault 30* (Hinchas de Poesía Press, 2022) and translator of Facundo Soto's *Juego de Chicos* (Jitney Books, 2018).